WHAT HAPPENS AFTER

a DI Wednesday novel

HEMMIE MARTIN

Winter Goose Publishing
45 Lafayette Road #114
North Hampton, NH 03862

www.wintergoosepublishing.com
Contact Information: info@wintergoosepublishing.com

What Happens After

COPYRIGHT © 2016 by Hemmie Martin

First Edition, February 2016

Cover Design by Winter Goose Publishing
Typesetting by Odyssey Books

ISBN: 978-1-941058-41-1

Published in the United States of America

Also from Hemmie Martin:

The Divine Pumpkin
Attic of the Mind
In the Light of Madness
Rightful Owner
Shadows in the Mind
Garlic & Gauloises

For my friend,
Gina Davis

Chapter 1

Against the backdrop of an ochre-tinged sky, The Davenport Hotel cast a jagged shadow on the pavement.

Jack and Michelle Turner were the last couple to arrive that Friday morning. They were shown into the gaudy guest lounge by a stout, ruddy-faced woman, who looked more suited to working on a farm than owning a hotel in Cambridge. Three more couples sat in the lounge, silently avoiding eye contact with one another.

"Thank you, Eileen," said a man in a paisley shirt and designer skinny black jeans.

Eileen Potter nodded curtly before leaving, closing the door firmly behind her.

"Welcome to our very first Parting Ways weekend. I'm Carl Trott, a facilitator, and this is my colleague, Stella Hibit, also a facilitator," he said, gesturing to his right.

Stella smiled, casting her gaze over the individuals. The group smiled cautiously, some coughed pathetically.

"As there will be times when you'll all meet up, such as mealtimes and group sessions, we thought you could all introduce yourselves. How about you start," Carl said, looking in one man's direction, who at fifty-seven was the eldest person in the room.

"I'm Vincent Vine, and this is Sandra. We've been married for thirty-three years." He glanced in her direction, to see her staring out the window.

The rest of the group mumbled a greeting.

"I'm Jack Turner, and this is Michelle." His manner was matter-of-fact; his voice clipped, encouraging only a smattering of low-key responses.

"My name's Paul Hart, and this is my . . . this is Megan." His face reddened as he shuffled in his seat.

"Some of you probably recognise me, or my voice, to be precise, from the radio. I'm Richie Dover, and this is Isobel."

Each introduction was perfunctory, resulting in a swift and frosty meet-and-greet.

Rubbing his hands together vigorously, Carl stood up. "Perhaps you'd all like to see your rooms before Stella or I meet you in your pairs." Moving to the lounge door, he called to Eileen.

In the harsh fluorescent light of the ladies' toilets, Wednesday poked and pulled the skin around her eyes. Giving up smoking had improved the clarity of her skin, and the dark circles under her eyes had melted away, but the lines remained on her face, like squatters.

Returning to her office, she found Lennox hovering outside her door.

"May I have a word?"

She ushered him through, closing the door behind her.

"I know Scarlett's a banned topic, but I just wanted to tell you I've been straight with her, and I won't be dating her anymore."

"And she's fully aware of that fact, is she? No room for misunderstanding?"

"Absolutely not."

"Did you say it's because of her mental illness?"

"I avoided the topic, and just said I'm not ready to be in a committed relationship."

"Good. I don't want to be clearing up your mess; you know how she is."

"I'll just go and finish the Jasper case report then, Boss."

She nodded, watching him retreat to his office; noticing some of the female staff gazing longingly in his direction. His effect on them had not dwindled over time, which made her smile.

Isobel Dover unpacked her weekend bag, brushing the creases from the clothes before hanging them up. All the items were new, as most of her other clothes were tainted by the memory of Richie, her soon-to-be ex-husband.

Closing her eyes briefly, she saw him in bed with another woman, writhing around in heated passion; the image folded her stomach causing her to heave. Hatred and disgust rattled around her mind, what little she had left of it, as motherhood had mashed her brain, according to Richie. He constantly reminded her of that fact, and she had now come to believe it.

Knowing his room was only a few doors away made her want to scream and claw at his face until raw nerves and twitching muscles were exposed. To counterbalance her anguish, she placed a framed photo of their two-year-old daughter, Holly, on the bedside cabinet. She had to do right by her, failure was not an option.

Later that evening, a game of musical chairs ensued as the group shuffled around the large oval table in the centre of the dining room. Spouses desperate not to sit together organised themselves until eventually the women sat at one side of the table, and the men sat at the other. It wasn't long until the women were talking to each other in hushed tones, whilst the men fiddled with the cutlery and the starched white napkins.

They all felt drained after their second day with the facilitators. Feelings of resentment were aired, names were called, and hurtful words were banded around, until they could no longer bear to make eye contact with the biggest mistake of their life. The close proximity of their poor choice in mate sent ripples of anger through the air, making the room a claustrophobic haven for malice.

When the young waiter, Hugo Frost, entered the room, he commanded the attention of every woman, as he did wherever he went. He moved effortlessly around the table, taking the drink orders, and leaning in closely to the women.

"I need a smoke," said Richie Dover, pushing his chair back.

"The doors are unlocked, sir," Hugo advised, pointing in the direction of the French doors.

Stepping outside, Richie pulled his jacket around him before lighting his cigarette and breathing in the toxic smoke. He wished he were anywhere but there, but in one more day he would be free from his oppressively clinging wife, leaving him free to trawl through the line of women throwing themselves at him in the nightclub.

Early Sunday morning, the individuals trickled down for breakfast, feeling the trepidation of the next onslaught of emotional flagellation awaiting them.

To save the room being swamped by negative silence, a radio played softly in the background; low enough not to niggle the minds of those people nursing a hangover.

"I didn't think I was hungry," Michelle Turner said, spooning fresh grapefruit and orange segments into a glass bowl. "But seeing all of this has swayed me."

No one responded to her, but she was used to that.

Everyone sat down at separate tables, not wishing to converse with one another after discussing their inner thoughts in the group session yesterday.

With ten minutes to go before the final sessions, Isobel scanned the room, noticing Richie was absent.

"Has anyone seen Richie?" she asked.

The women shrugged and the men shook their heads.

"Could you go and check, please. I don't want him to miss our session," she asked Hugo, who was refilling the bread basket.

He left and returned quickly. "He's not answering the door. Is he a heavy sleeper?"

"No. Can't you just go in and check on him?"

"What's the problem?" asked Eileen, entering the room carrying a large vase of flowers.

Hugo enlightened her. She sighed and promptly disappeared upstairs, her ample hips swaying with every stair she mounted.

"He's not in his room. Have you checked the garden?" she said sharply, on returning to the group.

"I'll go and check," offered Vincent, keen to get away from Sandra's constant forlorn look of disappointment.

The women talked in hushed tones about their experiences of marriage, speaking just loud enough in parts for the men to hear the odd disparaging word.

Vincent returned swiftly, bumbling through the French doors, panting for breath whilst miming the action of making a phone call.

Eileen was the only one paying attention to him.

"What-on-earth's the matter?"

He stood there, wide-eyed and glistening with sweat.

"For God's sake, man, spit it out," she snapped, causing everyone to stop and stare, before turning their attention to Vincent.

"He's dead . . . in the garden . . . dead . . ."

Isobel clattered her cup into the saucer, sloshing tea onto the white tablecloth. A silent scream echoed around her head but the tears failed to swell in her eyes. She felt numb, and was aware of being scrutinised by her fellow guests.

"I must see him," she uttered, standing up.

"I'd advise you against that, love, it's not a pretty sight," Vincent urged.

"Why?" she asked, her voice cracking.

"He's been stabbed, and there's a lot of blood."

Gasps rippled across the room as Eileen scampered off to call the police, fearing the impact on the reputation of her hotel, and ruing the day she agreed to take on these guests, against her better judgement.

"I'm going to take a look," announced Paul, a nurse who worked in A&E.

Isobel remained seated, clutching her mottled neck with her hand. Megan simultaneously placed one hand on Isobel's shoulder, and the other on her arm, whispering words of support.

At that moment, Carl and Stella rushed into the room, having been enlightened by Eileen.

"I suggest no one go near the crime scene; the police will need to see it untouched," Carl stated, moving towards the French doors, and closing them, unaware Paul had already slipped out.

Stella hovered in the background, twisting a signet-ring around her little fat finger. She turned to Eileen and requested a large pot of tea, to which Eileen huffed loudly before leaving the room.

Muffled sobs punctuated the silence as they waited for the police to arrive. No one looked in Isobel's direction, for fear of needing to offer words of condolence, or some such platitude. When the doorbell rang, a collective sigh traversed the stifling atmosphere.

"DI Wednesday and DS Lennox, may we come in?"

Eileen let them in, taking them to the dining room where expectant faces gazed up at them, like infants in a school assembly waiting to be given an achievement certificate.

"This is Isobel Dover, his wife," Carl Trott said.

"Very sorry for your loss. We'd like to speak with you in private, after we've viewed the crime scene," replied Wednesday.

Isobel nodded, still clinging onto a sodden tissue in her hand.

Carl took charge and led them into the garden. He paused and pointed in the direction of the roses.

"I believe he's over there. I really don't want to see a dead body, if you don't mind."

"No worries, thank you," Wednesday said, stepping swiftly towards the area.

The detectives found the body quickly.

"He was wise not to want to see the body," Lennox said, grimacing.

Chapter 2

Richie Dover's body lay on the manicured lawn, with his upper body in the border of rose bushes. A struggle had clearly taken place, as broken branches hung dejectedly from some of the bushes.

Edmond Carter, the pathologist, strolled up behind them.

"Ah, I see the cause of death may not be that difficult to ascertain," he said, kneeling down beside the body.

"Not sure which wound you're looking at?" replied Lennox.

"At first glance I'd say the stab wound to the chest."

"And I'd say the other wound makes this crime more personal, or just plain vicious," Wednesday commented, taking a closer look.

"Or someone wanting it to look that way. Was he alive when that happened?" whispered Lennox.

"I wager this was done post-mortem blah-de-blah . . ." Edmond muttered.

"Thank God for small mercies," Lennox said, doubling over in a gesture of pain.

"Time of death may require tests back at the lab, as rigor mortis may not be reliable if the body's been out overnight."

Suddenly they were surrounded by police officers cordoning-off the crime scene. Wednesday asked that a cast be taken of the footprint in the soil before they left Edmond to finish seeing the body in situ.

Eileen had reluctantly provided her office as the interview room, and it was there they met the fragile-looking Isobel Dover. She sat upright, with her hands clasped firmly in her lap; her eyes red and glistening.

"When did you both arrive here?" asked Wednesday.

"Friday morning."

"And the purpose of your stay?"

"We'd come to get divorced," she smiled wryly. "I know how that must look, but if you speak to Carl or Stella, they'll let you know about the ethos behind the Parting Ways weekend."

"Was this a mutual agreement?"

"Of course."

"So your marriage was over in both of your eyes?"

"Absolutely."

"Was there a reason?"

"Infidelity . . . his not mine."

"Was he wearing any jewellery?"

"A gold watch his father gave him for his twenty-first. He's never without it."

Wednesday could not recall a watch.

She looked at Isobel and remarked how her raven hair and wide green eyes gave her a doll-like innocent appearance.

"Did he have any problems at work?"

"No, everybody loved him, especially the women."

"That sounds like it was a problem for you."

"As I said, his infidelity is why we're here."

"Perhaps there are angry husbands scattered around?"

"I wouldn't know; I spend my time at home with our child." She blew her nose then sighed deeply.

"I'll get a family liaison officer to sit with you, if you'd like."

"I'm fine with the women here, thanks; they feel like my sisters."

Wednesday nodded, releasing her from the room, to re-join her newly-forged sisterhood.

"I'd like to speak to the leaders of this event, then the owner of the hotel."

Lennox arose and disappeared, before returning with Carl and Stella.

"This is a terrible thing to happen on our first Parting Ways weekend," Carl said, plonking himself down in a worn green leather chair.

Stella sat down more demurely.

"Could you explain how this weekend works?" Wednesday asked.

Carl sat back, inter-lacing his fingers. "The idea began in the Netherlands. Couples who aren't caught-up in a bitter dispute can spend the weekend in a hotel, and come out divorced at the end of it. All they need do is present the paperwork to the courts to finalise it."

"How do custody battles and financial affairs get sorted out?" Lennox asked.

"We try and get them to settle the issues amicably, but we also have a team of professional people available online; solicitors and estate agents to name a few, who will answer their queries, and guide, or represent them if required."

"We're here to ensure the wellbeing of both parties," Stella piped up.

"What about the sleeping arrangements?" queried Wednesday.

"Separate bedrooms, all on the same floor, however."

"Did you notice anyone arguing with the victim?"

"They'd only known one another for a couple of days; hardly time to dislike someone so much you'd kill them," Carl said, irritated by the question.

"I can be annoyed by a stranger sitting at the adjacent table in a pub after only five minutes," Lennox said.

"That says more about you than the stranger," Carl retorted, smiling broadly, dimples forming in his cheeks.

Lennox pursed his lips, puffing air down his nostrils. "How many times have you run these weekends?"

"As Carl said, this is our first, and it's not a very auspicious start," Stella said towards Wednesday.

"Has it put you off?" Lennox persisted.

"One would think, but I imagine we'll hold another, if Eileen agrees to it," she replied, pointedly ignoring him and looking at Wednesday.

"We'll see her next, if you wouldn't mind sending her in," Wednesday requested.

Eileen entered, her mouth in a permanent pinched expression with vertical lines converging between her unruly eyebrows.

"I imagine you're very observant when it comes to people-watching, with a business like yours," began Wednesday, placing her hands gently on her lap. "So I wonder if you could give me your thoughts on the group."

Eileen gave a curt nod. "I *have* been watching them, wondering what type of people would attend such an event." She paused to cough. "The women all seem to get along; moaning about their men, no doubt. However, the men aren't so friendly with one another."

"What are your thoughts on the victim, Richie Dover?"

"Slimy man. He seemed to have a roving eye."

"How did his wife respond to that?"

"She looked used to it; probably why they're divorcing."

"Did he upset the other men?"

"Honestly, call yourself an inspector. The men didn't care in the slightest, they all wanted shot of their wives, didn't they?"

Wednesday blushed. "You don't sound like you approve of this event."

"I don't like it at all, but this recession's hit me hard, so when they approached me with their idea, I had to accept their business. My poor Albert would be turning in his grave if he knew."

"What is it you find so difficult?"

"People don't try hard enough these days when a marriage hits hard times; they're too quick to give up and move on to the next person."

"Did you notice any bad behaviour or arguments between the couples, especially the victim and his wife? Perhaps you heard something during the late evening or night?"

"After dinner's been served, I go up to my apartment at the top of the hotel. I pay staff to keep an eye on things; I spend as little time around the guests as possible. And I can't hear anything from up there, thankfully."

She reminded Wednesday of a miniature schnauzer as she sat fidgeting in the chair; her grey-tinged, sparse-haired moustache twitching as she spoke.

"Who are your staff?"

"Tim Binder's the cook, and Hugo Frost tends to the bar, waits on tables, and manages the reception when I'm not around. All the women like to feast their eyes on him, I notice. I clean myself, as I haven't met anyone who comes up to my standards."

"That's impressive."

"I'm only sixty-six; I'm not at death's door."

Wednesday apologised quietly. "That'll be all for now, thank you."

At Wednesday's request, Lennox brought Vincent Vine to the room.

"How are you feeling after your shock discovery?" she asked.

"I've seen some sights in my life as a plumber, but that . . . Well, that will stay with me forever."

"Did you move or touch the body?"

"Not ruddy likely, it was easy to see he was dead. All that blood and the vacant stare in his eyes."

"How come you went looking for him?"

"Isobel was distressed he hadn't come down for breakfast, fearing he was going to miss their final session. I popped outside thinking he might be smoking in the garden like he's done before."

"When was the last time you saw him alive?"

"Around ten past ten Saturday night. He was going out for a smoke as I was going upstairs to bed. I'm an early sleeper, something Sandra always complained about in our marriage."

"Did you hear any strange noises during the night, or see anyone here who wasn't a guest?"

"I sleep deeply. Even a bloody loud noise from inside the bedroom wouldn't rouse me. Besides my bedroom faces the front of the hotel."

"Did you notice any animosity between Richie and Isobel during the day?"

"We've all got issues with our spouses, that's why we're here."

"I meant a deeper, more profound hostility."

"We're not supposed to talk about what others have said in group sessions, but I will say she was right to divorce him, in my opinion. She deserves better."

"What makes you say that?"

"He was a bit of a charmer with the ladies; he can't have been easy to live with. He couldn't help himself here, either, always having to give flirty eye contact with any woman in the vicinity."

Wednesday stored that away before thanking him for his time.

Next Sandra Vine sat opposite the detectives, assuming Vincent had bad-mouthed her. Wednesday swiftly put her straight, before turning Sandra's attention to Saturday evening.

"Last time I saw that man was at dinner time. He ate rapidly then went outside to smoke. He'd always request to have smoke breaks during the group sessions. He was obviously highly addicted, and it was annoying, not to mention smelly."

"What time did he go out for one?"

"He went straight after dinner then came back for coffee. The last time he went out was around ten; the news was just starting."

"Why do you refer to the victim as 'that man'?"

"He was a typical man; his actions were dictated by his trousers."

"Was he charming, in your opinion?"

"Too arrogant for me. Thought he was better than he was; he was only a local radio DJ after all."

Wednesday wondered whether anyone in the hotel liked the victim.

She decided to move on to the staff members next. Remembering

Eileen Potter's words about Hugo Frost, she was keen to see what all the fuss was about.

Chapter 3

Hugo Frost swaggered into the room, quickly making eye contact with Wednesday; offering her his perfected smile.

"Before you ask, I didn't really know the guy, but I could tell he'd pissed off the others."

"What makes you say that?" Wednesday asked coolly.

"Well some of the men had warmed to him, I suppose. That Paul Hart seemed to find him amusing, but I could tell all the others hated him."

"Any particular reason?"

"You'd have to ask them."

"When did you see him last?"

"He came to the bar around eleven for a Jack Daniel's. The bar closes at eleven fifteen and I leave at half past."

"Was he alone?"

"Jack Turner was there too."

"Did you go straight home?"

"Only to get changed, then I met some mates at the snooker club."

"If you think of anything else, just call us," she said, handing over her card before dismissing him.

"So do you find him attractive?" Lennox asked.

"Apart from being woefully too young for me, I can see the appeal, although he's too clean-cut for me."

"So I'm in with a chance then?" he grinned, rubbing his goatee.

"Ha-bloody-ha."

The chef, Tim Binder, was nowhere to be found, sending Eileen into an apoplectic meltdown as lunchtime was almost upon them.

So as not to waste time, the detectives moved on to Jack and Michelle Turner, finding it surprising they wanted to be interviewed together.

"I'm here to support Michelle; this event has rocked her to the core," Jack said, sitting on the chair next to her.

"That's very supportive seeing as you're both here to get divorced," Wednesday commented.

"I don't hate her; I've just fallen out of love with her."

"What brings you to this event then, if your divorce is amicable?"

"When two people fall out of love, their possessions become paramount to each of them. We both love the house and the dog, and neither of us is prepared to let them go to the other." Michelle's tone was clipped, her voice nasally.

"The supervised sessions are to help us work things out, without spending a fortune on solicitors," added Jack, forcing a smile.

"Whether we manage it remains to be seen. Thus far the sessions have only just scratched the surface, and now this murder's got in the way."

"It's all about you, isn't it? You've become so self-centred in your maturing years," Jack hissed through gritted teeth.

She flashed a glare at him as the tension mounted in the room.

"When did you last see Richie Dover?" asked Wednesday, eager to move things along.

"I went upstairs after dinner, to read my book in peace," said Michelle.

"I had a night-cap with him around eleven. We talked about what fools we were letting our wives talk us into coming to this event."

"You thought it was a good idea too," Michelle said indignantly.

"Did you enjoy his company?" Wednesday continued.

"Not particularly, he was a man's man, if you get my drift?"

"Not really," Wednesday quipped.

"He had affairs with numerous women he met in nightclubs, thought he was a lucky devil and all men were envious of him."

"Whilst his wife stayed at home with their two-year-old daughter," Michelle added.

"Okay," Wednesday interjected, "that will be all for now."

The pair walked out, taking the frosty air with them.

"Two more people to go, then we can head back. Any news on Tim Binder's whereabouts?"

Lennox scanned his mobile. "Arlow sent me an e-mail saying he's not in his flat, and get this, he's an ex-con. He was a hired thug, beating up victims for cash."

"That's a far cry from murder, though."

"Agreed, but it would be an easy step-up if the money was right."

"Let's leave the rest of the team to find him, and crack-on here."

"I could do with a coffee."

"I doubt Eileen Potter will run to that."

A knock at the door announced the arrival of Paul Hart, and Wednesday wasted no time in starting to question him.

"When did you last see the victim alive?"

"At the last group session. He was mouthing off about how women with children focus only on their kids and no longer on their own bodies or husbands. He certainly annoyed the female contingency."

"What did you do after the session?"

"I went to a veggie restaurant in the city centre. The cook's idea of a vegetarian meal here is a cheddar cheese salad."

"What did you think about the victim?"

"I wasn't here to think about other people; I was here to disentangle my life from Megan's."

"I understand you checked the body when Vincent found it. Did you move it?"

"I'm a nurse, so I just checked for a pulse, but I could see he was long gone, no point in CPR. I didn't move him, and I was surprised how queasy I felt, so I walked around the garden, which is why we missed one another, I guess."

"Where do you work?"

"At the Winter Bridge General Hospital in York."

"You've travelled far to come here."

"It's the only place of its kind in the UK, and I was keen to see if they could make divorce as easy and painless as they promised."

"And can they?"

"We may have been getting there, but this murder's halted any further progress."

"You seem sad about your situation."

"Megan and I were student nurses together. Things were great until she opted to work in a private clinic. She nurses people who've elected to have surgery on their faces and bodies for cosmetic reasons; it makes me sick."

"You're divorcing over that?"

"I'm a political and principled man; she's become materialistic and alienated from my world, not that it's any of your business."

"You both seem rather different from the other guests."

"Because we're young or because I have tattoos?"

Wednesday smiled, thanking him for his time, and requesting for Megan to be sent in.

"I have nothing significant to tell you, detectives. He was a lecherous man, and I'm not surprised someone killed him," she announced, sitting down.

"Why?"

"I imagine there are plenty of husbands out there wanting him dead. He boasted openly about his ability to pull any woman he wanted, even here."

"What does Isobel do when he's like that?"

"Sometimes she leaves the room and one of us will accompany her upstairs, or she remains in the room and stares out the window."

"Does your bedroom overlook the garden?"

"All of the women's bedrooms do. The men are opposite us."

"Did you hear anything last night?"

"Not after the amount of red wine I drank."

Wednesday sensed her clam-up, whether through indifference or fear, and knew that pushing her would yield nothing more for now. Megan left without uttering another word, leaving only the scent of freesia hanging in the air.

"None of the women heard a thing from the garden, but all of them disliked him intensely, so would they have responded if he had called out?" Lennox said, standing up to stretch his legs.

"Your guess is as good as mine. Let's get back to the station, I need a coffee now."

"I need a smoke too."

"I feel liberated now I don't smoke; you should give it a try."

"You promised not to badger me about it."

Wednesday smiled and shrugged as they made their way to the car.

Later that evening, Isobel opened her bedroom door to find Stella standing there with a bottle of wine in one hand, and two glasses in the other.

"Thought you'd like some company," she said, stepping inside without waiting to be asked.

Isobel wondered where they would sit, only to find Stella already on the bed, smiling broadly, and patting the space beside her. Isobel felt the heat rise in her cheeks as she moved towards her.

Wednesday and Lennox descended into the bowels of the building to see Edmond Carter. They found him hunched over the victim's body, muttering to himself.

"What have you got?" Wednesday asked.

"There's evidence of blunt-force trauma to the right side of the skull, possibly resulting in concussion. I would suggest something like a spade." He moved the head to expose the bruising behind the right ear. "The blow was from behind, so that would point to a right-handed assailant." He then shuffled down to be level with the chest area, pulling back the green sheet.

Wednesday shifted back subtly, leaving Lennox to peer intently at the wounds.

"There's a hesitation wound just above the stomach, see how it's only one centimetre in depth. The fatal wound was to the heart. The width, thickness, and depth of the wound points to a heavy-weight generic classic hunting knife; fifteen-inch single blade. There are two teeth missing from the serrated edge, which should help in identifying the weapon."

That gem was something Wednesday always hoped to get, but rarely had the satisfaction.

"Then we have the wound to his genital area, or should I say detachment of," Edmond continued.

Lennox grimaced seeing the genitals in an evidence bag on the metal table.

"This was done post-mortem, but it was hacked off awkwardly, not severed cleanly."

Lennox was impressed by Edmond's ability to be unmoved by such graphic details.

"His entanglement with the rose bushes left his forearms and hands with a plethora of scratches, which may also be evident on the assailant if you're lucky."

"That would be too good to be true," Wednesday smiled, her shoulders relaxing as he re-covered the body.

"I estimate the time of death to be between eleven and one o'clock in the morning."

She thanked him before returning upstairs, leaving Lennox to pace the courtyard alone with his cigarette.

"Any updates on Tim Binder?" she asked Arlow, passing his desk.

"Not as yet, but every force in the adjacent boroughs has a photo of him. He'll have nowhere to hide soon."

Wednesday wandered back to her office and began pushing sheets of paper around her desk, grouping people together and only coming up with two obvious factions: men and women.

She knew if you put a group of women together in one room, they would often reveal secrets and indiscretions through gossip and chit-chat. She called through to Damlish and asked him to organise such a meeting for the following morning.

Chapter 4

"Normally, I'd consider meeting these women without you; the sisterhood and all that. However, they're all in failing marriages, and I think you'll be a morale booster," Wednesday said, pulling into a space outside The Davenport Hotel.

"Glad I have my uses," Lennox quipped.

Hugo Frost showed the detectives into the guest lounge, where Michelle Turner, Sandra Vine, Megan Hart, and Isobel Dover awaited their arrival.

"Thank you for meeting us," Wednesday began, "we know this is a difficult time for all of you, especially you, Mrs Dover."

"I'm well supported here, but I'm not sure how this meeting is going to help find his killer," she replied softly.

"Let's start at the beginning. You all independently reported a dislike for Richie, and we were wondering how he'd managed to offend you all?"

All the women looked towards Isobel, as if awaiting some sort of sign. When nothing came, Sandra Vine spoke.

"When a man is married to a beautiful and kind woman, who gave birth to his child only two years ago, he's supposed to treasure her, not jump into bed with other women."

"I understand an affair is an emotive subject, is it a common theme with you all?"

"No it isn't, and I don't see what business it is of yours?" Sandra sniped.

"Then it doesn't fully explain your dislike of him?"

"Sisterhood," piped up Megan Hart, her cheeks glowing.

Wednesday eyed Lennox fleetingly.

"So you all hate each other's spouses as vehemently as you do your own, in support of one another?" he asked, looking around the room with his sharp hazel eyes.

"If more men were like you, I'm sure there'd be less hate in the world," Michelle Turner said, coquettishly.

"Honestly, Michelle, you've no idea what he's like. He could be a philandering swine like the rest of them, for all you know," Sandra spat. "Don't embarrass yourself by throwing yourself at him; you look pathetic."

Michelle blushed furiously and waited for someone to come to her defence. When her discomfort was met by a wall of silence, she tutted theatrically, clenching her fists in her lap.

Sandra folded her arms and huffed loudly. "Don't all look at me like that; I was only stating the truth, something none of you do."

"Perhaps we should return to the topic of Richie," said Megan. "Why don't you talk about him, Isobel, it might be therapeutic."

"This whole weekend was supposed to be therapeutic, but so far I've only felt humiliated and shocked."

"Why humiliated?" questioned Wednesday.

"Because not only was he constantly unfaithful, his last conquest was only seventeen. Do you know how gross that made me feel? My body never regained its pre-birth firmness, and all I could think about was him in bed with a seventeen-year-old taut body." She visibly shuddered.

Wednesday swallowed hard. "How did everyone find out about it?"

"We all attended a sharing session on Saturday afternoon," began Sandra, clearly taking charge again. "Each couple aired their dirty linen, something I was opposed to, but I was overruled. Anyway, when Richie admitted his faux pas, we women were all shocked. But the men . . ."

"They thought he was a lucky dog," interjected Isobel.

"All except Jack; I think he has a soft spot for you, in a fatherly-way, you understand," Michelle said, turning to Isobel.

"What makes you say that?" Wednesday asked.

"The way he looks at Isobel. I think he'd have liked a daughter like her."

"He felt protective of her?"

"I suppose so."

"Would he do anything to carry out that action?"

Michelle's eyebrows twitched. "Jack wouldn't be capable of violence, if that's what you're implying. He's incapable of being demonstrative."

"Is that part of the reason for your divorce?"

Michelle sighed. "You're determined to dig, aren't you?"

Wednesday smiled lightly.

"I've come to realise just how much he's stopped noticing and caring for me. Our love has shrivelled over time. We both love our dog more than each other."

"Can we go now?" asked Megan, fidgeting in her seat. "I'm uncomfortable re-hashing our marital failures with you. Richie's dead, and I'm sorry for Isobel, but we didn't hear or see anything that can help you."

Lennox thanked them, making Michelle blush and look at him from under her canopy of false eyelashes. Wednesday smiled to herself.

As they filed out, Wednesday leant in to Lennox and suggested he round up the men, to see exactly how they felt about the victim.

Unlike the women, none of the men took charge of the group, preferring instead to sit with arms folded, and neutral faces. That was until Wednesday asked them how they felt about Richie Dover's affair.

"Personally I think if the opportunity to sleep with a seventeen-year-old arose for any man in this room, we'd all jump at the chance," said Paul Hart.

"Speak for yourself," snapped Jack.

"Oh come on, none of us would turn down the offer," goaded Vincent, rubbing his hands together.

"It's disgusting; a seventeen-year-old is still an adolescent. It smacks of dirty old man syndrome." Jack's face glowed with perspiration. "He was sad and pathetic; an embarrassment to men in general."

"What do you think, Sergeant?" asked Paul, turning towards Lennox.

"I'm not here to discuss my views on the matter," Lennox replied.

"You seem vehemently opposed to Richie's idea of an affair. Is it to do with the affair per se, or her age?" asked Wednesday.

"Her age of course," spat Jack. "She's someone's daughter."

"Or yours had things been different." Wednesday studied his face hard, watching for every nuance of emotion. "Apart from his affair, how did you all get along with him?"

"We were the closest in age, and so had the most in common," replied Paul. "I tried to convince him to give-up smoking, but he said it was his only joy in life, apart from his work."

"Was his life that bad?"

"He said Isobel had changed since having the baby."

"He wasn't getting enough attention?"

"No, apparently she'd turned to drink."

"Did you notice her drinking excessively whilst here?"

"We've all been drinking; it's a symptom of our situations," Jack chipped in. "We're lining the landlady's pocket with the price she charges for alcohol too, if you ask me."

Paul coughed. "He was one of us; a man on the brink of regaining his freedom. We all supported one another, just as the women clubbed together against us."

"It had become a battle between you all? I thought the facilitators were here to prevent that," Lennox queried.

"They did when they were here, but they left at six in the evening, leaving us plenty of time to bicker." Jack was composed once more, the lines on his face less crumpled.

"Thank you for your time, gentlemen, we'll leave you to bicker in peace." Wednesday could not help passing the comment, knowing that professionalism had snuck under the carpet for a brief moment.

"I'd like to discuss our findings with the facilitators. See what they have to say about the cauldron of emotions they leave behind at the end of the day. Let's get back so you can arrange the meetings," she said to Lennox, who was fondling a packet of cigarettes in his pocket. "You can have a smoke first, if you must."

Lennox nodded before hastening outside.

"Why did you force me to reveal Richie's heinous act?" Isobel complained to the women as they all sat with a cup of tea in hand.

"It was bound to come out," replied Sandra. "Anyway, why does it matter?"

"The investigation should be about Richie's murder, not about what led us to this place."

"Oh grow up; the police aren't interested in your dull past."

"You can be such a bitch at times." Michelle stood up and strode to the fireplace. "I'm not surprised Vincent wants to divorce you."

"Low blow," Isobel said quietly.

"Get your facts right, you stupid cow. I'm the one doing the leaving, in exchange for a life of freedom and peace."

Both women were on their feet, staring each other down from a few paces away. The sound of their jagged breathing cut into the atmosphere like two dogs preparing to fight. Isobel coughed as she rose to speak.

"Please let's not do this to one another. I need all of you to be there for me. I'm dreading going back to the empty house . . ."

"You were getting divorced, so what's the problem with an empty house?" interrupted Sandra.

"I knew he'd still be around for Holly and in case of emergency. But this way he's gone forever."

"God you lot are weak," Sandra hissed, before leaving the room and heading for her bedroom.

"I've arranged for us to meet Carl Trott at his home," Lennox said to Wednesday as she stuffed a chunk of chocolate into her mouth.

"Great, I'll drive."

Carl lived in a townhouse in the centre of Cambridge. Two bicycles were chained to a metal post by the front door. On ringing the doorbell, the sound of tinny chimes filtered through the door.

A waif-like woman opened the door and peered at them for a few seconds.

"Sorry, I've misplaced my glasses. I'm Tamara, his girlfriend. Come in, he's waiting for you," she said, pointing up the flight of stairs straight in front of them.

Carl stood at the top, hands in pockets, rocking on the balls of his Italian leather-clad feet.

They followed him into a stark gleaming-white kitchen-diner and sat around a large glass table.

"Richie Dover appears to have caused quite a male-female divide, with the exception of one male," said Wednesday, shifting in the unforgiving metal chair.

"I assume you've learnt the age of his conquest," Carl replied, his hands clasped on the table.

"What impression did he give you?"

"Cocky, arrogant, showy, all the unappealing characteristics of a man who's used to getting what he wants."

"Did he argue with anyone during the two days?"

"Apart from with Isobel, no, I don't think so. Although, come to think of it, Stella found him rather challenging."

"Why was that?"

"I don't know exactly; you'd have to ask her."

Tamara walked over to the table with white china mugs of coffee, placing them in front of everyone.

"I'm worried about Carl being there after dark," she said. "Do you think there's a maniac there?"

"We don't think there's a serial killer, if that's what you mean," reassured Lennox.

"I told you not to worry about me," Carl said, putting his hand on hers.

"What are the women like? Are they all falling over themselves to spend one-to-one time with Carl?" she asked Wednesday directly.

"Is that what usually happens?"

"Women usually become interested in him when they know he's a counsellor. They imagine he can read their minds and offer them wise words. I think they equate counsellor with being warm, gentle, and caring."

"Tam, you're reading too much into things. She always thinks women come-on to me when we're out. It's simply not true."

"He thinks I'm blind or stupid. They practically drool over him; drowning in his forget-me-not blue eyes."

The atmosphere cooled around the table, with only the steam from the coffee adding some semblance of life to the stagnant air.

"Jack Turner didn't applaud Richie's act. Did you witness an altercation between them at any time?" Wednesday asked.

"Look, I can see what you're getting at, but quite frankly, none of the group seem capable of committing murder, it must be an outsider."

"There's no evidence of a break-in." Wednesday took a sip of coffee, savouring the depth of flavour. "The owner, Eileen Porter, doesn't seem enamoured with the type of service you offer."

"She's old-school and believes people don't work hard enough at marriage, and to some extent she has a point."

"But wouldn't that negate this part of the job you do?"

"We're there to make the split as amicable as possible, not work miracles."

"Do you sometimes find that one member of the couple wants to try and work it out?"

"Sometimes, but not in Richie and Isobel's case. He wanted his freedom to do as he wished, and his infidelity was too hard for her to overcome. In fact, she was finding it hard to be amicable over any issue, especially when he put in for sole custody of their child."

Wednesday sat up. "How come?"

"On account of her drinking. He professed she was an alcoholic, but I have to confess, I didn't notice any tell-tale signs."

"So you think he was making it up?"

"Prove it or not, just the mere hint of it makes judges nervous; the child's welfare is paramount, after all."

"How was that affecting Isobel?"

"Ironically, it made her anxious, and she took to having a few glasses of wine to calm her nerves."

Wednesday looked across at Tamara, and noticed she was gripping the mug so tightly, her knuckles had turned white.

"Did you ever meet her?" Wednesday asked.

"I'm not sure, I might have."

Carl looked puzzled. "When would you have done that?"

"I called in Friday evening looking for you. You hadn't come home and your mobile was off."

"I have my own counselling sessions then, had you forgotten?"

Tamara nodded.

"Did you meet them all?" asked Wednesday.

"Perhaps, I don't know. I went into the bar area, and quite a few were having a drink."

"Was Richie Dover there?" Wednesday asked, showing her a photo of the deceased.

"I believe he was sitting at the bar, boasting about how many young women he could have once free of his shackles, as he put it."

"Who did you speak to?" queried Carl.

"Just the bartender, Hugo, is it? I didn't tell you when you got home, as when I remembered where you were, I didn't want you to think I'm stupid."

"You must feel able to share, Tam; secrets could rot our foundation and shake us apart."

Lennox rolled his eyes, bringing a subtle smile to Wednesday's lips.

"One last thing, where were you both Saturday evening?"

"Here, together, watching a film," replied Carl.

The detectives left, feeling they had unearthed a Second World War bomb in a crater, for Carl and Tamara to dispose of as safely as possible.

Their next stop was Stella Hibit.

Chapter 5

Stella's abode was dour from the outside in contrast to Carl's pristine and manicured exterior. The cracked concrete path leading to the door was lined with wheelie bins belonging to the eight flats; all numbered with white paint that had run in places.

Lennox pressed the buzzer and spoke into the intercom. A shrill sound spewed out as the door unlocked.

The lift was poky and smelt of underarm sweat and stale tobacco, forcing Wednesday to place her finger under her nose.

Stella's front door was covered with stickers depicting various breeds of cats in a variety of poses.

"Oh great," muttered Lennox as Stella opened the door.

"Come in quickly, Rollo loves to roam the landing, but the neighbours complain," she said, almost pulling them inside.

Wednesday found the flat smelt little better than the lift.

Stella led them to the lounge, a rectangle room with a corner sofa, two club chairs, and coffee table at one end, and a dining table and four chairs at the other. Two of the cats were curled up in a fabric basket, with the third cat sprawled out over half of the sofa. Wednesday and Lennox took a chair each, leaving Stella to negotiate space with the fat cat on the sofa.

"We understand you found working with Richie Dover rather challenging," said Wednesday.

"I suppose Carl told you that. He found my distaste at the man hilarious."

"What was it you found so unpalatable?"

"The affair with such a young girl, of course. I hated the way he flaunted his success with younger women. He had a beautiful wife, and gorgeous daughter, and he threw it all away for the lust of younger flesh."

"Have you seen their daughter?"

"Only in a photo Isobel took to the hotel."

"Isobel doesn't appear as affronted as some of you are. Why is that, do you think?"

"She *is* deeply upset, which she divulged on a one-to-one basis. She's not one for sharing much in a group or displaying her emotions publicly."

"Have you seen her much on her own?"

"Just the Friday evening; I could tell she needed to talk."

"Did you witness any tension between Richie and the others?"

"There were two distinct tribes, the men and the women. I would say there was overall tension between the tribes rather than individuals."

"Where were you Saturday night?"

"Here, with only my cats to vouch for that, I'm afraid. I did order a pizza around seven thirty, if that helps."

Wednesday smiled, thanking her for her time before leaving with Lennox in tow. They took the stairs at Wednesday's insistence.

"She gave the impression of being very single, didn't she?" she asked as they climbed into the car.

"Very much so. Why?"

"Just wondered if I've glimpsed into my future."

"I doubt it. You just need to be less, picky, dare I say?"

"You dare not," she replied, pushing a Joni Mitchell CD into the player and slamming the car into reverse.

Lennox screwed up his face, forming a map of his gathering lines.

"What was that all about Friday evening?" Carl asked Tamara, as she cleared away the mugs.

"As I said, I wondered where you were, that's all."

"You're letting yourself be ruled by negative thoughts again, aren't you?"

"Is there any wonder? You forget I know what you're like and what you're capable of. I have every right to worry."

He sighed. "I don't want you coming to the hotel again. You're being paranoid, and you know where that can lead you, don't you?"

Tamara dumped the mugs into the sink with a clatter before rushing upstairs, locking herself in the bathroom, and bursting into tears.

"You can let the guests at the hotel return home; we've nothing to keep them there," Digby Hunter told Wednesday as she was checking her mobile.

She shoved it back in her bag. "Yes, Guv. They all live in Cambridgeshire, except for the Harts who live in Yorkshire, so travelling's not a problem."

"How are things with you?" he asked.

"Fine."

"Is that the sum total of your life?"

She felt herself blush. "Work takes up the majority of my life, not that I'm complaining, you understand." She smiled meekly.

"You should get out more, Eva. You're too young to be rotting away at home in your free time."

"I wasn't aware I was rotting," she laughed, "but thanks for the heads-up."

He hesitated a second before returning to his office.

"We thought it would aid closure, for some of us, if we all ate together for our last evening here," Carl said, placing his hand on Isobel's shoulder.

She looked up at him and smiled, her cheeks a gentle hue of raspberry.

"This weekend's been an unmitigated disaster; and seeing as I'm not leaving a happily divorced man, I assume a refund's on the cards," said Vincent.

"Not exactly. Mrs Potter needs to be paid for your time and food here, and Stella and I also have bills to pay. We thought we'd offer one third of the fee back, except for you, Isobel, you don't have to pay at all." He looked around the table.

"That's not really good enough," Sandra retorted. "You didn't deliver what you promised."

"We didn't anticipate one of the guests being murdered," interjected Stella. "We understand your feelings, really we do. If you wish to participate in the next event, we'll offer you a fifty percent discount."

Mutterings crackled across the room as she sat down.

"At least we aired some of our pent-up feelings," Paul said, before picking up the pint of beer in front of him.

"But nothing's resolved. I still find Vincent insufferable," Sandra snapped. "We'll still need to pay a solicitor to get the job done."

"We have contacts, we'll ask them to offer you a discount, as a gesture of goodwill." Carl's face was dotted with beads of perspiration.

"Now perhaps we should move away from this topic and spend a moment thinking about Richie Dover, and his widow, Isobel," Stella said quietly.

"At least she got what she came for," hissed Sandra, who received a quick kick from Vincent under the table.

Hugo breezed into the room, carrying four plates of duck pâté, which he placed in front of the women. Michelle Turner looked up, fluttering her lashes and thanking him.

A while later after the meal, everyone hung around the bar, too afraid of being alone. Hugo charmed the women into buying more drinks, including ones for him.

"What are your plans now?" Megan asked Isobel.

"I'll return to the house and be with my little girl. I'm a single mum now," she sighed.

"With the mortgage paid off, no doubt, plus any life insurance," Sandra said bitterly.

"You truly are a fountain of fucking joy, aren't you?" Vincent spat. "You'll never find another man once I'm gone."

"Thank heavens for that; after living with you, I'd rather live in a convent than with another man."

"Can't you two be civil just for our last evening together, out of respect for Richie?" asked Paul.

"Like he was worth respecting," Jack sneered from a corner of the room.

"As admirable as your protection of Isobel may be, perhaps now is not the time," Stella said quietly.

"This is a highly emotive time. I suggest we finish our drinks before heading up to our respective rooms," chipped in Carl.

Stella seconded the motion as they all finished their drinks in silence and parted ways.

As each bedroom door closed, Hugo picked up his mobile and pressed speed dial.

Pushing her plate to one side, Wednesday spread out the beginnings of her mind map over the table, chewing on a pencil as her eyes roamed the paper.

Richie Dover was almost universally disliked, and several people may have wished him harm. But to carry it out, that took real courage, or real hatred, and she was not sure if any of them had much of either.

The weapon did not materialise during the search in the hotel or garden, and photos of the type of watch and engraving detail had only just been sent to local pawn brokers. Her own increased impatience irritated her, as she knew it also did Lennox; a legacy of giving up smoking.

Removing the pencil from her mouth, she got up to make an Earl Grey tea, feeling the silence of her home acutely. Scarlett had returned to her own place since her relationship with Lennox had petered out, but Oliver had kept her informed of Scarlett's increased mood swings, making them both worry about her medication compliance. She sighed as she took her cup of tea and a novel upstairs.

Hugo carried Isobel's suitcase downstairs, whilst she followed behind in a lighter mood than when she had arrived. The rest of the guests were paying their bar bills at the reception. Everyone turned as she drew level with them.

"I'll be perfectly fine," she said, addressing them all. "I've had a good night's sleep and I feel positive this morning. You must all now sort out your own lives in the way Carl and Stella have shown us."

The group muttered, and Sandra uncharacteristically bit her lip.

"I'm pleased you have a positive attitude, Isobel; Holly will need you to be strong," Stella said, from the doorway.

Isobel smiled in her direction as her taxi arrived to take her home, to the other side of Cambridge.

Eileen Potter watched the group as they trickled out of her hotel.

"What a repugnant group people," she said, shoving their cash in the till.

"It's money though, Mrs P," Hugo replied.

"I know, but it doesn't feel good having that sort here."

"What have you got against them?"

"Didn't you hear about the one who died? He'd slept with a seventeen-year-old; wouldn't surprise me if it was his wife who killed him, and I wouldn't blame her."

"She was legal."

"You're missing the point; at seventeen you're still a child, and he was most definitely an adult, there's a power imbalance. It's abhorrent."

Hugo frowned. "Sounds like you wouldn't have minded killing him yourself."

"Watch what you say, idle words cause trouble. Now go and strip the beds."

Arlow tapped on Wednesday's door.

"Got some interesting news, Boss. Children's Social Services have a file on the Dovers. Apparently, Richie Dover did inform them of Isobel's drinking and inability to parent adequately. They are due to visit her within the next ten days."

"I think Lennox and I need to pay her a visit."

Chapter 6

"Someone keeps calling the home phone and hanging up when I answer. Is there something, or someone, you're not telling me about?" asked Tamara, throwing the apple core into the food waste bin.

"Probably just some reporter trying to get a juicy story from me. They hear your voice and hang up," replied Carl.

"Why don't they just ask for you then?"

"I don't know; why don't you ask them?"

"I have, but they don't reply."

Carl shrugged, returning his attention to his laptop.

"I hope you haven't done anything stupid, because I don't want to be dragged into it. So whoever they are, get them to stop calling." She glared at him before stomping downstairs with her cycling helmet and slamming the front door behind her.

Isobel Dover answered the door with little Holly clinging to her legs.

"You have news?"

"More questions, I'm afraid," Wednesday replied.

Isobel hoisted Holly up and let them in before closing the door.

"We've learnt that Children's Social Services are to pay you a visit within the next ten days," Wednesday said, sitting down on a cream leather sofa.

"So what? Richie did that out of spite, and it's all academic now he's dead."

"Are the allegations unfounded?"

"Of course they are."

"Why would Richie choose alcohol as a vice?" Wednesday asked, looking around the pale mauve-and-cream room.

"Easy one to say, I suppose."

"They will still investigate even though he's dead; a child's welfare is paramount."

"I would never harm Holly; she means the world to me." As if to prove it, she bounced her on her knee until the child wriggled wildly to dismount.

"What happens to the house now?"

"He made a will and everything goes to me. He never got the chance to change it. I suppose that weighs against me."

Wednesday tilted her head to one side. "Did your husband have a laptop?"

"Yes, I presume you want it?" Without hesitating, she rose and put Holly down before leaving the room.

Holly wandered over to Lennox. He smiled at her and showed her his warrant card, which she looked at with wonderment. She held it in her chubby little hands, and waved it around, laughing as she did so. Wednesday saw him wistfully watching her.

"Here it is," Isobel said, holding the laptop in her hand. "I don't know what you're looking for?"

"Neither do we, but our experts might find something pertinent," Lennox replied, taking it from her and giving her an evidence slip in return.

Lennox took the laptop to the technical team before heading for the courtyard for a lonely smoke.

Wednesday found Damlish hovering around her office door.

"Boss, Richie Dover's watch has turned up in a pawn shop. I checked out the CCTV and found what looks like a male bringing it in. He's wearing a baseball cap low to hide his identity. The shop owner couldn't describe him."

"Or wouldn't. Anyway, it's a start. See if forensics can get any prints from the watch."

Entering her office, she pulled a chocolate bar out of her desk drawer, and sat down. Through her glass partition she saw Lennox return; she missed their moments in the courtyard, the smoking bond between them.

An officer entered Lennox's office then disappeared, only to return with Michelle Turner in tow. Lennox greeted her before walking over to Wednesday.

"She wants to talk with me, but I thought you should sit in too."

The three of them entered the interview room and sat down. Michelle sat opposite Lennox at an angle, cutting off Wednesday as much as possible.

"I felt compelled to come and see you," she said, looking directly at him. "It's about Jack." She pulled on her earlobe, making the diamond stud sparkle in the artificial light. "Did he tell you he went outside for a smoke with Richie on Saturday night?"

"He didn't," replied Lennox. "Was there something else?"

"I heard him come up to his room late. I was going to ask him what they'd been talking about when I heard him come out of his room to go to the bathroom."

"What's unusual about that?

"He went to have a shower, and I found that odd, don't you? Do you think he was washing blood off his body?"

"That's an enormous leap from having a smoke with the victim, to murdering him. Why would he murder Richie?"

"Even though we're divorcing, he's still very possessive of me, and Richie was very flirtatious." She toyed with her necklace as a blotchy red rash dappled across her cleavage. "Also, he was strangely over-protective of Isobel. The fact that Richie had an affair with such a young woman really riled him."

"Do you remember what he was wearing that evening?"

"Not particularly, but knowing him it would have been a pale pink or stripy polo shirt and beige chinos. He's so predictable and boring," she sighed, looking at Lennox from under her eyelashes.

"Thank you for coming forward with this information," Lennox said, standing up.

"Is that all?" Her eyes widened. "I thought you'd need to ask me more questions."

"We need to ask Mr Turner some questions now, but we'll get back to you if need be."

"I do hope so," she smiled, touching his arm as she rose.

"You've got a fan there," Wednesday said, watching the woman sashay down the corridor.

Lennox grunted. "I'll drive to Turner's."

Jack Turner's face turned crimson on opening the door to the detectives, a springer spaniel leaping around his feet.

"We'd like to ask you a few questions," Wednesday said.

"Can't it wait? You can see I'm dressed for golf."

"It won't take long," she replied, stepping forward.

Sighing, he stood back then took them straight into the kitchen, where they all took a seat around the large table, in the centre of the duck-egg-blue room. The dog followed them excitedly, eventually settling in his tartan bed.

"You didn't mention going out for a smoke with Richie Dover the evening he was murdered," she said in a measured voice.

Silently, he contemplated his answer, before looking at her directly.

"I suppose I have Michelle to thank for that."

"Why did you conceal this fact?"

"Isn't it obvious? It made me the last person to see him alive, and in the garden where he was found dead."

"The information was bound to come out sooner or later. You'd have been wiser to be upfront, as now we wonder what else you could be lying about."

Scraping his chair back, Jack stood up and began pacing the room.

"I fancied a cigar, that's all. I wasn't interested in talking to him; it had been a hard day and I wanted to get away from Michelle."

"What did you talk about?"

"I just said I didn't want to talk to him."

"Maybe so, but I can't see you two standing together in silence," she persisted.

Jack stopped in front of the window, gazing onto his much-loved garden. "He talked, I merely listened. He said it was unfair how everyone was so against him for the affair, because of her age. He said all the men were envious of his position."

"Is that how you felt?"

Puffing out his cheeks, he turned to face them. "I admit his action grated on me, but not out of jealousy. An affair damages a wife, but more so if she's spurned for a much younger woman."

"And that concerned you how?"

"I just felt sorry for Isobel; she didn't deserve it."

"You seem protective of her, why is that?"

"I suppose I imagine if I'd had a daughter she'd have been like her."

"What did that do to your feelings towards Richie?"

Now gripping onto the back of a chair, he leant forward, his face glistening with sweat. "Okay, I admit, I felt angry towards him; it's men like him who give the rest of us a bad name."

"Did you act on these emotions?"

"I felt like punching the smirk off his face, but I didn't. I smoked my cigar half-way down before stubbing it out to take it back inside. He was alive and unscathed when I left him."

"Did he mention he was worried about anything or anyone?"

"He only said he was worried about leaving his daughter in the care of Isobel."

"What were his concerns, exactly?"

"He said Isobel was an alcoholic, and believed she'd have a string of men so Holly would grow up with loose morals."

"What did you say to that?"

"I said I couldn't believe that of her, and he said she had me fooled, along with everyone else she came into contact with. He called her a master manipulator."

Wednesday looked around the kitchen. "You have a very nice home."

"My estate agent business pays for all of this. It's the house and Jasper," he said, looking at the dog, "that Michelle and I are fighting over. Glad we didn't have kids." His gaze fell to Jasper, who was curled up with his head on his tatty toy.

"Thank you for your time. We may need to speak with you again."

Smiling forlornly, he showed them out, the dog once again at his feet.

"It's difficult to know whether Isobel really is alcohol dependant, or whether they were words forged out of a bitter divorce," Wednesday said, sliding into the car seat.

"Maybe we should investigate her more closely," he replied, fumbling with the cigarette packet in his pocket.

Tamara Jackson swallowed the tablet, forcing it to not stick in her throat like her sentiments had. After her visit to the hotel, she suspected something was not quite right. Richie had paid for his sins, and now it was Carl's turn.

Chapter 7

"Niall's wants me to get some more news on the murder in that hotel," Scarlett said, passing the gravy boat to Wednesday.

"Your editor knows better than to ask for that."

"Come on, it's the first divorce hotel in the country, which is a story in itself. But it's all gone quiet regarding the murder."

"That's what happens in a murder enquiry; it's not blood, guts, and action all the way to the denouement."

"Not a conversation for the table," Joan chipped in, swirling her wine in the bulbous glass.

"Sorry Mum. How are pottery sales, Oliver?" Wednesday asked.

"Slow but steady. I'm currently designing a new pattern for a breakfast set." Oliver looked enthused behind his tired eyes. Wednesday believed she was the only one who saw his true emotions, which he guarded well from the others.

"Are you painting, Mum?"

"I've started a new canvas, but inspiration is evading me once more."

Wednesday offered an encouraging smile. The atmosphere was fragile, and she wanted to get out as soon as possible, before it stained her mind, leaving vein-like threads of black tar seeping imperceptibly through her brain.

Carl Trott picked up the post strewn across the door mat. Most was for Tamara except for a blue envelope. He slit it open and read the letter.

"Something wrong?" Tamara asked, coming down the stairs.

"No," he said, stuffing it into his pocket. "I've got to get to work, I'll see you later." He donned his cycling helmet and left.

Wednesday put the receiver down after speaking to Children's Social Services. Doodling on the notepaper, she ruminated over the information provided, before calling Lennox to her office.

"Social Services have interviewed Isobel Dover, and were surprised at her affability during the interview. She assured them she was only a social drinker, and Holly engaged well with her, so they're closing the case," she informed him. "However, what Jack Turner told us Richie said about her, seems incongruous. Perhaps we should get another viewpoint; let's visit Stella Hibit."

Stella appeared from her office with a patient in tow. After another appointment was made, the patient left as Stella walked towards the waiting detectives.

"I have a half-hour lunch slot, if you don't mind me eating my sandwich at the same time."

Her office was light and airy. Long windows were swathed in lacy off-white nets, which flew like ghosts in the breeze. The bright interior was complimented by two cream armchairs, and a painting of an empty beach on a summer's day.

"We'd like your professional opinion on Isobel Dover," Wednesday said, sitting down in one of the plump armchairs.

Stella retrieved her cellophane-wrapped sandwich from her drawer, and proceeded to peel it off.

"I suppose seeing as she wasn't a patient of mine, but part of a couple for the divorce weekend, I can speak freely up to a point."

"We appreciate that. We've been given two very different views of her personality and we'd like to know what you think."

"Well, without knowing what's already been said, I'd say she was a calm, measured, and tolerant woman, who juggled running a home and being a mummy very well, considering her husband's string of infidelities."

"Did you find her manipulative in any way?"

Stella took a bite of her sandwich, before covering her mouth to speak. "I didn't see any evidence in the two days I worked with her and her husband. I suppose those were his words regurgitated by someone else in the group."

"How did you find her in Richie's company?"

Stella shrugged. "They were like many divorcing couples; both bitter, but she had good reason to be as he was a philanderer and not much of a father, by all accounts."

"*All* accounts?"

"Just a turn of phrase, really. I spoke with Isobel on her own a couple of times; she was quite cut-up about his last indiscretion."

"The seventeen-year-old?"

"She just about coped with the other women he met at the nightclubs, but the age of this one made her question what he saw in her post-baby body. Her self-esteem had taken a terrific blow."

"Was she happy to be getting a divorce? Perhaps it wasn't her idea?"

"It *was* her idea, although she wasn't happy about it. All she wanted out of life was a secure and loving home for Holly. He threw that all away, and she was angry with him."

"Angry enough to commit a crime?"

Stella choked on a breadcrumb. "You can't believe she killed him. Over what?"

"Over the custody of their child. Were you aware that her husband had accused her of being an inadequate mother due to drinking too much, and was seeking sole custody?"

Stella paused. "Yes, but his claims were preposterous; she didn't drink more than any of us in the hotel. I guess he fabricated the barbed story just to hurt and punish her."

"Was there a consensus from the others that he was lying, or was there just a male, female divide?"

Stella screwed the cellophane into a ball before tossing it in the wicker bin. "The men didn't really express much on an opinion, except I could tell Jack was more concerned about Isobel's welfare. I'm sorry, but I need to start preparing for my next patient. I hope I've been of some help."

"Thank you; we'll get back to you if need be."

They stood and moved to the door, before Lennox turned and spoke.

"Did you meet the couples prior to them staying at the hotel?"

"An insightful question, detective. We did meet the prospective couples who applied for the event, to check their suitability for the programme."

As they headed for the car, Wednesday asked him what made him ask that question.

"Not sure, really. It may add nothing to the case, of course."

Wednesday found the lull in the Incident Room disconcerting. Leads on the case had withered, and she desperately wanted something fresh to stimulate her mind into action.

On her way over to make a coffee, she paused at Arlow's desk.

"Any news on the whereabouts of Tim Binder?"

"Someone matching his description was seen in a pub in Leeds, but by the time officers got there, he'd gone."

Wednesday tutted before moving away. Watching the liquid swirl into a vortex in the mug as she stirred it, she failed to notice Hunter move up behind her.

"I hear Scarlett Willow's been in The Crazy Duck trying to find someone who'll talk about the Dover case."

Wednesday felt herself blush before eventually turning around to face him.

"That's the first I've heard of this. You've got to hand it to her, Guv, she's not lacking in drive and resourcefulness."

"Regardless of how you feel about her journalistic tenacity, I'd like you to warn her off such blatant actions."

Wednesday wet her mouth with a sip of steaming coffee.

"I'll mention it to her, but she'll say the pub's a public domain."

"She can drink there if she must, but fraternising with officers about any case is off-limits, understood?"

"Yes, Guv."

He strode off, closing his office door firmly behind him, leaving Wednesday to stew in a new-found resentment for her half-sister.

Returning to her office, she poured over the notes of interviews, trying to find a common denominator to point her in a certain direction. As she began drawing a mind map, Lennox knocked on her door.

"A knife's been found in a wheelie bin not far from the hotel. Alex is examining it as we speak."

"At last, that's great. Meet you there in ten," she said, opening another chocolate bar.

Wandering into the bowels of the building, she bumped into Lennox coming in from the courtyard, reeking of smoke. She wrinkled her face, holding her finger under her nose.

Alex Green was hunched over the knife on the table, dusting it down for prints.

"Got anything for me?" she asked.

"Hello to you too," he quipped with a smile. "I've only had it for a short while. It's been wiped down, so no discernible prints. What I can tell you is it's a heavy-weight, classic hunting knife, fifteen-inch blade, with two teeth missing. Need to check with Edmond, but my guess is it'll match the wounds on the body."

"So this is the weapon, but no leads from it," Wednesday said, staring at it, willing it to reveal its secrets.

"This is commonly for sale in the right shops, plus it looks quite old,"

Alex added, "so no leads there. You could find out who likes camping or hunting as a starting point."

"Let's go hunting ourselves," Wednesday said, bounding up the stairs.

Wednesday and Lennox arrived at Isobel Dover's house unannounced.

"Is it important? I have a visitor," she said, pulling the door behind her.

"We'd like to ask you a few questions. We could do it in another room for privacy," offered Wednesday.

Grimacing, she directed them to the lounge, which they found empty.

"What kind of holidays did you and Richie like?" Wednesday asked.

Isobel frowned. "Strange question."

"All the same, could you answer it?"

"We had plenty of fabulous holidays before we had Holly."

"What kind?"

"Mainly city breaks, Richie liked fine dining and wine bars, and I like museums."

"Either of you into camping?"

"Good God no. I need running water and a proper mattress, plus Richie liked to look his best at all times. You can't do that in a tent."

"There's something else I'd like to ask," Wednesday said, leaning forward. "Your husband mentioned to some of the guests that you manipulate people around to your way of thinking; you always get people to see you in a positive light."

Isobel huffed a staccato laugh. "Bitter words from a man who couldn't bear to be spurned. I was supposed to accept his affairs and keep playing the good little wife and mother. It was he who was trying to turn people against me. He was the master manipulator." Her eyes shone like puddles in the moonlight.

A movement in the doorway caught Wednesday's eye.

"Is everything all right in here? Isobel sounds distressed," Stella said, entering the room.

"We didn't realise you were the guest Isobel mentioned," Wednesday said, arching an eyebrow.

"I was worried about her emotional wellbeing, so I called in, that's all." She moved to sit next to Isobel on the sofa.

"It's funny, even though Richie and I were divorcing, his death's hit me hard. I suppose I'm upset for Holly not having a father anymore." A single fat tear tumbled down her hollow cheek.

Stella placed her hand on Isobel's and gave a gentle squeeze.

"They're doubting my character. Apparently, Richie told someone in the hotel that I manipulate people. It wasn't you, was it?"

"Certainly not."

"Whilst you're here," Wednesday said, turning to Stella. "What type of holidays do you go on?"

"I like to rent isolated cottages in places like Derbyshire or The Cotswolds. What's that got to do with anything?"

"They asked me too," Isobel said in a squeaky voice.

"We've found what we think is the murder weapon."

Isobel gasped, putting her hand over her mouth.

"But what's it got to do with holiday destinations?" queried Stella.

"It's a hunting knife."

"Hardly use for one of those around here. How macabre."

"Sorry if I've upset you, Mrs Dover. We'll see ourselves out." Wednesday rose and Lennox followed.

"Let's go back to the hotel and see if any of the staff have a penchant for camping or hunting," she said, sliding into the car seat.

Chapter 8

Bright blooms filled the two hanging baskets outside the hotel, but they didn't detract from the grubby facade.

As Wednesday and Lennox entered, Eileen Potter grimaced.

"I thought you were guests. As gruesome as it seems, some people want to stay where a murder took place."

"Gruesome indeed, but not surprising. We'd like to ask you a few questions," Wednesday replied.

Eileen took them into her private lounge which was overrun with potted plants, and bird ornaments.

"Do you ever get the chance to take a holiday?" Wednesday asked.

"Not for years, well not since my husband died eight years ago."

"That must be hard. Do you have any camping equipment in the hotel?"

"Whatever for?"

"Would your late husband have had the need of a hunting knife, at one time or another?"

"Gracious no. The closest he got to hunting was bird watching in Wales."

"What about guests or visitors to the hotel?" Lennox asked.

She rolled her eyes. "No one has ever asked me about hunting or camping locally."

"Is Hugo Frost on duty?"

"He is, and maybe he's the camping connection you're looking for."

They wandered into the reception area, where Hugo was filling the leaflet stand.

"Could we have word?" Lennox asked.

Hugo's ears turned red as he faced the pair. Lennox asked similar questions to the ones Eileen answered, but again, they were disappointed.

"What do you do in your spare time?" Wednesday asked, flicking through leaflets of local attractions.

"I tend to hang out with friends, play pool, and go to clubs."

"Any of them into camping or hunting?"

He paused, rubbing the back of the neck.

"Does that ring a bell?"

"Some of the guys used to go camping by the river Cam, but that was years ago. They'd rather go clubbing in Ibiza now."

"Have any of them visited this hotel?"

He laughed. "Mrs P would never let my mates in here."

The telephone rang taking him away from them.

"Hunter won't be impressed by our lack of progress," Wednesday sighed. "But maybe we need to spread the net wider. Let's get the names of his mates, see where that takes us," she said, nodding in Hugo's direction.

Just as Hugo had predicted, his friends were gathered in the pool club hovering around a green-topped table.

It was only early afternoon, but the young men were already drinking pints of lager, making them obnoxiously loud. No one noticed the detectives walking up to the table until Lennox put his hand over a pocket, preventing a ball from dropping down it.

"Hey old man, what the fuck you doing?" spat an acne-scarred youth.

"What's your name, son?"

"What's it to you?"

"We're detectives investigating a murder at The Davenport Hotel."

"Leroy Evans, and we ain't murdered no one. We've never even been to that hotel."

"We're not saying you have. We're just exploring everyone who's linked to The Davenport Hotel," Lennox said, pulling his notebook from his pocket, "and you're all mates with Hugo Frost. Let's save time, lads, and just give me your names."

The three young men swaggered around the table, and Leroy introduced them.

"Matthew Cummings and Damien Philpot."

"So how do you all know Hugo Frost?"

"We all went to college together, a catering course."

"Have you all got jobs?"

"Matt and I haven't, but Damien works in a fish van outside here every Friday night."

"Not one of you has visited the hotel where your mate works? Not even to meet him after work to come here?"

"We've already said no," retorted Damien Philpot. "Hugo says his boss is a dragon, and wouldn't allow us in anyway."

"He told us you used to go camping by the river. Do you still have the equipment?"

"We didn't have much in the first place, it was more sleeping rough, smoking, and drinking cider," Leroy sneered. "Anyway, we haven't been for a few years, I doubt we could find any of the gear."

"Okay lads, thanks for your help."

"That was pointless," muttered Lennox, climbing into the car.

"Not like you to be so negative, what's up?"

"I'm moving to a two-bed house especially so the boys can stay over, but Lucy's not allowing me to have them overnight, saying they have homework to do."

"You could help them with that, surely."

"I said as much, but she said I have a poor record at being helpful and reliable. I'm being treated like a malevolent teenager."

"Just concentrate on building a relationship with your boys, and forget the rest, it will soon follow."

The journey to Ely took the detectives along a scenic route. Wednesday watched the fields blur into one another in the distance before dense hedges obscured her view. On the other side, a train whipped along the horizon, and ahead, the spire of the cathedral stood erect above the flat land.

They arrived outside the Vine residence; a robust semi-detached house, with an unnecessarily long front garden. The wrought-iron gate squeaked as Wednesday opened it, and the path was slippery with moss.

Sandra opened the door and let them in; the air smelt of dusty carpet.

"You can see Vincent after you've spoken to me; I refuse to be in the same room as him."

"Are you no further forward with your divorce?" Wednesday asked, perching on the edge of the hairy sofa.

"I want to go through solicitors, but he refuses to pay for it. That's why we were at the hotel." A cat jumped onto her lap and nestled into her.

"There are lots of photos of children around the room."

"We have four sons, all grown up. Two are engaged, one is married and expecting our first grandchild, and our last son is in the army."

"Did you bring them up in this house?"

"We did. We had to extend it to cater for the children though."

"I notice lots of photos taken around a campfire."

"Vincent was, and still is, a scout leader. He took us all on scout trips; they were the only holidays we had and I hated every one of them."

"Does he still go camping?"

"He does, but thank heavens I don't have to. I love it when he's away."

"Could we see Mr Vine now please?" Wednesday monitored her voice, wanting to hide her urgency.

Sandra left the room and hollered up the stairs. Movements were heard from above, as Vincent padded around.

He arrived looking dishevelled, rubbing the top of his shaved head. Wednesday did not hesitate in asking him about his camping trips.

"Sandra been moaning about our family holidays, has she?"

"I understand you're still a scout leader. Do you have your own camping equipment?"

"Of course, a scout always needs to be prepared."

"What about a hunting knife?"

"Yes . . . Oh I see, was that what the murder weapon was?"

"Do you know where yours is?"

He paused, licking his dry lips. "All my equipment is kept in the attic, including the knife."

"We'd like to see it, please."

"What, now?"

Wednesday stared at him until he stood up, rolling his eyes before returning upstairs.

Wednesday wandered around the room, studying the photos closely. The sons seemed captivated, and Vincent beamed proudly from centre stage. Sandra was either on the periphery, looking vacant, or not there at all, probably taking the photo.

Heavy footsteps announced his return; balls of fluff and spider webs clinging to his polo shirt.

"This is rather awkward; I can't find it." He shrugged, shoving his hands in his trouser pockets.

"What condition was it in?"

"As it should be, sharp and clean."

"I'd like you to keep looking for it, please, then bring it to the station. If you take too long, I may get a search warrant."

His face turned puce as the pair walked past him; he pressed his lips together until they felt numb.

On arriving at the Turner residence, the detectives found only Jack at home.

"She's at work," he said sharply.

"We'll find her later, but we'd like to ask you a few questions,"

Wednesday replied coolly.

He hesitated in the doorway.

"We can ask you questions out here if you want, but it would be more private inside."

Begrudgingly, he let them into the square hallway that was cluttered with a plethora of tweed and leather jackets. Above the telephone was a photo of Turner standing in a river in waders, holding a rainbow trout.

"You're a fly fisherman," Lennox said, peering closely at the photo.

"It's the only place I can hang the photo. Michelle hates the sight of fish unless it's battered on her plate. Heathen."

"Do you go camping whilst fishing?"

"Yes, I revel in the whole outdoors experience. Michelle used to come with me, but now she prefers spa breaks. They don't make her look any better though," he sniggered.

"Would you have use for a hunting knife?"

"I use a knife to fillet salmon on the bank before frying it to eat. There's nothing tastier."

"Is your equipment to hand?"

"A keen fisherman yourself, are you?"

"We just want to see the knife."

They followed Jack to the garage, where he opened up a metal cabinet to reveal his rods, nets, boxes of handmade flies, and his camping equipment. It was so organised, he pulled out the knife instantly. It was not the type of knife they were looking for.

"Thanks for your time," Lennox said.

"Be careful when you interview Michelle," he said directly to Lennox, "she's sweet on you."

Wednesday controlled her face until they left the house and got in the car.

"Don't say anything," Lennox said, looking straight ahead.

A call came in; they had found Tim Binder.

Chapter 9

The Incident Room was buzzing with the knowledge of Tim Binder's apprehension. Wednesday crammed a chunk of chocolate into her mouth before heading to the interview room with Lennox.

He sat in the chair, head bowed, with his arms hanging between his legs in a chimp-like fashion. His head remained low as they entered the room, and after taking their seats they waited, allowing the tension to build. He soon looked up.

"Do I need a solicitor?" he asked, in a heavy East London accent.

"Only if you're guilty of something. Why did you run?" replied Wednesday.

"I wasn't doing a runner, my ma was taken sick and I had to rush to her."

"Without telling your employer?"

"I knew she'd say no on account of having guests. It's family first with me, all the way."

"And how is your mother now?"

"Better."

"We'll need her contact details, so we can confirm your story," she said, suspecting his mother would vouch for him regardless.

"You must realise how suspicious it looks, you running away after a murder, especially as you're an ex-con."

"There you have it; you were bound to blame me from the start. Having form means you pigs never give me a chance; I'm always guilty in your eyes."

"If that were the case, you'd be arrested. We're interviewing everyone who was at the hotel, and we never got the chance to talk to you. It's as simple as that."

Tim slumped further into the chair, resting his chin on his chest.

"Where were you that Saturday night?"

"You know I was working," he spat, before catching Wednesday's eye and turning red. "I finished up about ten thirty then went home."

"Can anyone corroborate that?"

"I live alone; the wife left me after my last stint in prison, so no."

"From experience, you know that doesn't look good. You were in prison for being a hired muscle; you'd beat anyone up for money, isn't that right?"

"You know it is, but I was never hired to murder anyone."

"The offer of a large sum of money could persuade you."

"No, you've got it wrong. I ain't no murderer." His face was mottled with grey and red patches, and glistening with beads of sweat.

"We'd like to take a look at your bank account, if you don't object, see how the land lies. Still betting on the horses?"

"What if I am? It ain't against the law."

Wednesday stood up. "You can wait here whilst we do a few background checks." And with that, she and Lennox left the room.

She put Arlow and Damlish into action, before setting off with Lennox to speak to Paul Hart.

Paul was living in the nurse's home on the hospital grounds, until the house was sold, where Megan was still living.

Lennox breathed in deeply as they entered the building, and mounted the stairs.

"I've been to some wild parties in nurses' homes in the past."

"Why doesn't that surprise me?"

Paul opened the door, smiling wanly. "It's too small in here for all of us. Let's go to the canteen."

Only a smattering of staff and visitors occupied seats, enabling them to take a table in the corner, for privacy.

"This is better than living in a B&B," said Lennox, perusing the few nurses, and appreciating their uniforms.

"Not at my age. At twenty-five, I'm too old for a lot of their shenanigans. Their immaturity annoys me."

"Have you remembered anything else about that Saturday night, or the Sunday morning when you checked over the body?"

"The image is etched on my mind, but I don't remember anything else. No closer to catching who did it?"

"Do you have any hobbies outside of nursing?"

"Strange question," he said, blowing on his coffee. "I work in the emergency department, and I've seen how the police operate when questioning a suspect. What is it you're actually looking for?"

"Do you have the need for a hunting knife?"

"If you haven't noticed, I'm a veggie and a bit of a hippy at heart. Hunting repulses me."

"Could also be used for camping," chipped in Lennox.

"I don't camp; Megan's parents have a chalet in France . . ."

"Just dawned on you, you won't be going there anymore," Lennox grinned.

"Megan is entwined in bourgeois frippery, and she's finally succumbed to her parents' wishes by working in a private clinic, probably with the hope of her finding a rich man to ensnare."

"Obviously means a lot to you," Wednesday said, before draining her cup.

"Political differences are too big for me to overlook; I'm a man of principals. Believe it or not, we were both Labour Party members, and we'd go on Greenpeace marches. She's fallen so far. I'm sorry I can't be more helpful about the knife."

"Thanks for your time."

"We've only got Megan Hart and Carl Trott to go," Wednesday said, striding towards the exit.

It was turning out to be a long day, and by the time they got to Carl's house, it was late afternoon. Tamara opened the door wearing a floral apron, and brandishing a spatula.

"Detectives, this is rather bad timing."

"Sorry, the day's flown. Could we just ask you a couple of questions?" Wednesday asked.

"Who is it? Oh." Carl was crouching down at the top of the stairs.

"Just a few questions; we won't stay long."

Tamara led them to the kitchen where Carl was deftly chopping mushrooms, keeping his back to them at all times.

"I'll cut to the chase, do either of you own a hunting knife?" Wednesday asked.

Tamara spoke for them both, replying that neither of them had the need for such an implement. "We both love sport, especially skiing. Squash is another favourite." She busily stirred chopped onions in a frying pan.

"You've observed the group after the murder, Mr Trott. What do you make of their actions and reactions?" Wednesday asked, walking up to him to watch him chopping.

"That's not an easy question to answer in a short time."

"Carl could *bore* the pants off a stone statue when it comes to talking about psychology and the machinations of behaviour," Tamara smiled sourly.

Putting down the knife, he turned around and leant against the worktop. "Everyone was obviously shocked, and the women rallied around Isobel."

"How was she?"

"She looked composed at first, before breaking down uncontrollably. She kept saying she didn't want it to end like this."

"What did you take that to mean?"

"I presumed she meant she didn't want him dead. Divorce can be a civil event if worked through well."

"Did everyone remain in the dining room?"

"I believe everyone was there, well, apart from Eileen Potter."

"Was the cook there?"

"I wouldn't know what they looked like."

"Did anyone draw your attention by being more affected by the murder than the others?"

"Michelle Turner was being her usual drama-queen self; hoping to gain the attention of every male in the room, except for her husband's." He rolled his eyes. "The waiter-come-bartender looked rather pale and distracted. But he's young, so more impressionable I would say."

"You must have overheard gossip meandering around the group after we'd gone. People forming their own theories," Lennox smiled.

"Of course, but I don't partake in such activities."

Lennox just stared, raising his eyebrows.

Carl moved towards the table, pulling out a chair to sit on.

"Okay, Michelle Turner said she wouldn't be surprised if her husband had done it, to protect his *poor* Isobel, as she called her. Jack flew into a rage, whilst Isobel rocked in a chair, being comforted by the other women. All very Jane Austin."

Tamara sighed loudly, clattering the spatula into the frying pan.

"I suppose the women were trying to show Carl what compassionate souls they were," she said haughtily. "Women warm to him, believing he's an angel, not realising they're paying for his time, in essence, he doesn't give it away for free. I should know."

"I don't think the detectives are interested in the nuances of our relationship, Tam," he said, standing up and moving towards her; attempting to put his arm around her waist.

Tamara side-stepped away. "I think they should be aware that some women would do anything to get your attention."

"Who, for example?" Wednesday asked.

"Carl had a patient at his clinic, once, who self-harmed late at night to such an extent that he'd be contacted by the out-of-hours doctor, as she said only he could help her. And guess what? He used to go and see her at all hours. Her plan worked."

"Tam, my professional role is not on judgement here. They want to know about this group of people, one of whom was murdered."

"His wife could have done it to grab your attention. I bet you found her pretty, right?" she said, turning to Lennox.

"If you think of anything else, please give us a call," Wednesday said, brusquely handing Carl her card, and moving between Tamara and Lennox.

Carl led them out, muttering an apology at the door as they left.

"She's a scary woman," Lennox said, dropping into the driver's seat.

"Perhaps she has reasons for her behaviour; I'm not sure how I feel about Carl right now."

"You women always stick together."

"I'll ignore that, this day's been long enough. Let's head back; we'll see Megan Hart tomorrow, and see what gems she comes up with."

"That was bloody unnecessary and embarrassing," Carl said, returning to the kitchen where Tamara was scraping cremated onions from the frying pan into the bin.

"You've only got yourself to blame. They say history repeats itself, and if it does, the police will certainly find out, won't they?"

"Do we need to have a talk?" he queried, eyeing her carefully.

"I think I'm beyond the talking stage, don't you?"

"If that's how you feel."

"You're such a smug bastard at times," she replied, flinging the spatula at him. "I'm watching you. I won't let you leave me."

Carl brushed congealed onions from his top before grabbing his cycling helmet and leaving the house. Tamara ran upstairs, slamming the bedroom door behind her.

Chapter 10

Alex Green tapped on Wednesday's office door.

"Thought you'd like an update," he grinned, entering the room.

"Let's hear it then."

"The cast of the shoeprint has thrown up a match. It's a size nine, Adidas Original baseball cleat desert boot. Not cheap, one hundred and thirty quid." He showed her a photo of the boot.

"Doesn't seem the type of shoe any of the guests would wear."

"Maybe someone did get into the garden?"

"No evidence as yet and the garden's surround by a seven-foot wall."

"Glad I'm not an inspector then. Good luck," he said before returning to his lab.

She surmised the rumours were right; Alex must indeed be dating a girl from the admin office. He had finally got around to dating someone his own age, and Wednesday was touched by a moment of clarity and chagrin.

Megan Hart was still in her nurse's uniform when she answered the door.

"I'd forgotten you were coming; I've only just got in, but come in anyway," she said, stepping back, leaving a trail of freesia scent in the air.

It was an open-plan house, styled with a contemporary feel. The walls were painted a muted grey, and the picture frames and mirrors were chrome; sunlight bouncing off them.

"Have you found who killed Richie?"

"The investigation is still ongoing. Have you had any more thoughts about your time at The Davenport?" asked Wednesday, finding the sofa unyielding.

"I don't see who'd have a reason to murder him, except for his wife. Although, Jack didn't seem to like him much."

"What makes you say that?"

"He didn't have the time for him. When Richie went out for a smoke, he'd say, "It'll be the death of him, hopefully."

"That doesn't amount to much."

"You didn't see how much more relaxed Jack was when Richie left the room."

"Why do you suppose he didn't like the victim?"

"I don't know that; I'm just telling you what I saw."

"Where do you work?" asked Lennox.

"The Patterson clinic; I work on the plastic surgery side of the building, and occasionally in the private sexual health clinic on the other side."

Lennox noticed the family photo taken in front of a gîte. "Is that your family's place?"

"Yes, just outside Avignon. Do you know it?"

"I've only been to Lyon and Marseilles."

"I love the French way of life," she sighed. "I hope to live there one day."

"Any use for a hunting knife whilst you're there?"

"Heavens no. I'm all about topping-up my tan and eating copious amounts of olives and fresh peaches."

Wednesday and Lennox left Megan, and wandered to the car.

"Jack Turner's name crops up often. We've witnessed his anger, we know he owns a hunting knife, and his wife and Megan have nudged us in his direction," Wednesday said.

"His wife could be doing it out of spite."

"That goes without saying, but what would be Megan's motive?"

"Sisterhood?"

Wednesday shook her head. "There's something more obvious we're missing, and it's irritating the hell out of me."

Megan picked up her mobile and dialled, whilst pacing the room.

"The police have been here. I want to get away ASAP, so have you got the money ready?"

She listened for a few seconds.

"I'll give you three more days, but that's it." She hung up before wandering upstairs to shower.

"The police were crawling all over the hotel. Did they find anything?" Damien Philpot asked, picking up a pool cue.

Hugo shrugged. "Not that I know of. Why, are you worried?"

"Of course I'm frigging worried, aren't you?"

"Only if you did something stupid."

"I told you I didn't." He struck the white ball so hard it jumped over the edge of the table and rolled along the floor.

"Well, you've nothing to worry about then."

Chucking the cue on the table, Damien stomped over to the bar and ordered a pint.

Wednesday had just settled at her desk when her phone rang. She was informed there was an irate Jack Turner on the line.

"I've looked everywhere and I can't find it, you have to believe me," he said breathlessly.

"I'm sorry I'm not sure what you're talking about?"

"The bloody hunting knife, you wanted it, I don't have it. It's a mystery."

"Right, well, Mr Turner, all I can suggest is that you keep an eye out for it, but we may want to conduct a search, if we have sufficient cause."

"Great, now I have that hanging over my head." He hung up abruptly, leaving Wednesday listening to the dialling tone.

Lennox tapped on her office door, smiling as she looked up.

"Alex just gave me the results from the hunting knife, wiped cleaned of all prints, as we expected. But he did find tiny specks of dried blood matching Richie Dover."

"Jack Turner can't find his knife, but I'm not convinced it's him; it would go against his scout's honour," she smiled wanly.

"Alex normally contacts you; maybe he's finally got over his infatuation with you now he's finally dating."

She dipped her head and turned to the computer screen.

Isobel Dover bent down to pick up the post before wandering into the kitchen. Sunshine streamed through the window, catching the stained glass panel in the kitchen door, casting coloured shards across the bland vinyl floor.

She sat down with her mug of green tea and slit open an envelope before pulling out the letter. She inhaled sharply as she read the note.

Shaking, she retrieved her mobile from her bag and pressed speed dial.

"Sorry to trouble you, I need to talk, is now a good time?"

"Sure, what's wrong, you sound terrible."

"I've just received a foul letter, accusing me of wanting to be with Carl. They said they'll be watching me. It's not signed, but they say they saw me flirt with him. It must be a member of the group."

"That's awful, I'm so sorry. Would you like me to come over?" Jack offered.

"I can't ask you to do that, I just wanted to hear a friendly voice, and for you to reassure me that you didn't see me flirting with him."

"He's a good-looking guy; it wouldn't surprise me if you did."

"But I didn't," she cried indignantly. "I hate all men currently, except for you; you're like a father to me."

Jack coughed. "That makes me feel old. Now are you sure you don't want me to come over; I could go with you to the police."

"You think I should show them?"

"Naturally, someone's threatening you. If you don't feel safe at home, you could always come here."

"That's kind of you, but I don't think Michelle would appreciate having a two-year-old around the house."

"I'd like it . . . I could always camp out in your home. Look, think about it and I'll call you back tomorrow."

Isobel put her mobile down and pushed the letter away; it made her feel sick. Jack's words had done little to appease her troubled mind; instead, she mentally ran through all the guests at the hotel, trying to work out who was threatening her.

Turning around, Jack found Michelle standing behind him, red-faced, with the spaniel at her feet.

"So we're not even divorced yet and you're already picking up women, *that* woman to be precise, and moving her in here."

"Don't be so petty, she's having a rough time . . ."

"And you thought you'd smooth things over for her."

"Are you jealous of every woman in society, or just Isobel?"

"Oh grow up, I'm worth ten of her."

Jack laughed before stepping forward and slamming the door in her face.

"Don't you dare do that," she yelled, flinging the door open so hard, the handle dented the wall behind. "I still live here too, you bastard. Don't think I'll let you bring any whore into my home."

The dog barked, jumping up between them, excited by their raised voices and animated actions.

"Whore? You *are* jealous of her. Is it her youth, beauty, or genteel nature?"

"She's truly made an impression on you, hasn't she? Did you kill her husband to please her and speed things along?"

"You're babbling, woman; age has turned you into a crazy cow."

"You're the one closer to fifty, but you act like a seventy-year-old in bed," she screamed.

"That's your doing, you frigid old—"

His vitriolic stream was interrupted by the doorbell. Yanking it open, Michelle found Wednesday and Lennox standing there.

Chapter 11

"Are we interrupting?" Wednesday asked.

Michelle flattened her hair with the palm of her hand, smiling feebly. "Detectives, how can we help?"

"We'd like a word with Mr Turner," Wednesday replied, looking around her to see him standing in a doorway.

Jack led them into the lounge before closing the door firmly.

"Is this about the knife?"

"No, it's been found. We'd still like to see yours though."

"So I can prove the one you've got isn't mine. No pressure then."

"Actually, we want to ask you more about your time in the garden with Richie Dover."

"I only had a smoke with him. I don't smoke often as Michelle makes such a fuss about it. But that evening I was feeling a step closer to being free from her, so I smoked a cigar to celebrate, that's all."

"How did he seem to you? Was he anxious, nervous, agitated?"

"His usual cocky self, harping on how easy it was to get women in the nightclubs. He said they all loved a DJ."

"Did he mention having a problem with anyone?"

"Not that I recall."

"Did he return inside with you afterwards?"

"I got bored of his bragging, so I went back in alone. He was alive when I left him."

"Did you hear or see anything unusual whilst out there?"

"Nothing, no strange noises, and no one else was around. When I got in, the bartender was getting ready to go home."

"How do you know?"

"He was by the front door."

"What time was that?"

"I'm not sure. Perhaps just before eleven."

"Did he see you?"

"Can't say I remember."

They left the estranged couple to resume rowing.

"Another testament against marriage," Wednesday snapped, climbing into the car.

Hugo Frost's smile slid from his face on opening the front door to the detectives. He begrudgingly let them in, saying his mum was out.

"You told us you leave work at eleven fifteen, but someone saw you at the front door before eleven that Saturday night," she said, watching his eyes flicker.

"I wasn't leaving; I was checking it was locked."

Wednesday studied his feet, clad in black brogues.

"And you're sure you didn't see anyone else around?"

"Definitely sure. Have I done something wrong?"

"You tell us? You seem nervous."

"That's because you police always think young people are criminals."

"I don't remember saying that."

"So why did you go and question my mates then?"

"Spreading the net wide; nothing we don't do in other investigations."

"Well you can look elsewhere. If you ask me, the answer's in that group; bunch of weirdoes."

"We'd like to take a look at your shoes, if you don't mind."

"Don't you need a warrant?"

"We can get one, or you can assist in an investigation voluntarily, especially if you've nothing to hide."

He led them upstairs, stomping on every step and muttering under his breath. On opening his bedroom door, a faint whiff of feet from socks and trainers scattered around hit their noses.

"Typical boy's room," Lennox said, bending down to check for more trainers under the bed.

Wednesday started with the visible trainers, all expensive brands, but none matching the ones they were seeking, or the footprint. Moving to the wardrobe, she checked for more pairs, but only found expensive leather brogues and loafers.

"Work shoes," he said.

"Actually, I was wondering how you afforded all these expensive shoes and clothes," she replied, feeling the sleeve of a Paul Smith shirt. "Your job must pay well."

"It does, and I get tips. Now, if you haven't found what you want, I'd like you to leave before Mum gets back. She'll freak out if she finds you here with the house all messy."

They left him putting his trainers in the shoe rack, mumbling profanities to himself.

"Let's do the rounds of his mates before he gets the chance to warn them all," Wednesday said, fastening her seatbelt.

"What are you so agitated about?" Tamara asked, as Carl paced the kitchen.

"What makes you think I'm agitated?"

"Oh don't give me your counsellor speech, we're past that now."

"Well stop interfering in things you know nothing about."

"It's that woman, isn't it? Is she who you're planning on seeing behind my back?"

"Stop your paranoia from flowing, it's unattractive."

"But I bet she's attractive to you, with all her grieving and needy demeanour. I bet you can't wait to soothe her troubled soul. But be careful, she could be dangerous."

"Like you, you mean."

"Careful, Carl, you don't want to see how dangerous I can be."

He glanced at her before grabbing his jacket from the back of the chair and darting downstairs to the front door.

"Don't think I don't know what you really thought about Richie Dover. Watch your step, Carl, watch your step," she yelled as he slammed the door behind him.

Chapter 12

Tamara was putting her key in the front door when Wednesday and Lennox pulled up outside her house.

Sighing loudly, she let them in.

"He's not here, and I've just got in from work," she said in a clipped voice, mounting the stairs before slinging her bag on the kitchen table.

"It's you we want to see," Wednesday replied.

Tamara raised an over-plucked eyebrow.

"We've a letter here, sent to Isobel Dover. Would you know anything about it?"

Opening the fridge, Tamara pulled out a bottle of white wine and poured herself a glass.

"I could deny any knowledge, but as my fingerprints will be all over it, I might as well explain. Carl's a sucker for a damsel-in-distress, and I could tell she'd got her claws into him. The letter was warning her off, that's all."

"How do you know Carl's a sucker, as you put it?"

She took a large swig of drink. "I've been with him long enough; I know how he ticks."

Wednesday was unsure whether Tamara was going to add anything to their investigation, or whether she was just another jealous woman with low self-esteem.

"How did you know her address?"

"I found it in a file in Carl's study."

"Where did you and Carl meet?" asked Lennox.

"He's not told you, I suppose." She took another gulp, letting a slither of wine run along between her lips. "I was his original damsel-in-distress, you see, so I know how he operates."

"You were once his patient?"

She nodded. "So you see, I'm not paranoid thinking he could be attracted to another patient."

"That breaks his professional code of conduct," Wednesday said sharply.

"He's cleverer than that," she smiled. "He made sure my therapy was truly over before asking me out on a date. He's no fool, and he always gets what he wants in the end." She fell silent before getting up and refilling her wine glass. "Is there anything else?"

Wednesday requested Tamara cease communicating with Isobel, who had decided not to press charges, otherwise they would arrest her despite Isobel's views. Tamara smiled wryly before knocking back half a glass of wine.

Wednesday sat next to Scarlett and opposite her mother, as Oliver served the food.

"How's the pottery going?" she asked.

"It's going down well, and I've got five orders for teapots."

Wednesday smiled before catching her mother's eye. "And what about your painting?"

"Inspiration continues to elude me. I only want to paint black lines on white paper. Who'd want to buy that?"

In truth, Joan had not sold any paintings for a several years; gone were the days when inspiration outnumbered her dark days. Everyone knew it, including Joan, in her moments of insight.

"Aren't you going to ask me how I'm doing?" Scarlett whined.

"What's new with you, then?"

"I'm taking my meds, and I'm interviewing the owner of The Davenport Hotel tomorrow about the Parting Ways weekend. Both facilitators declined an interview. Their loss."

"Why doesn't that surprise me? Tread carefully, I don't want Hunter on my back."

"Oh why don't you just sleep with him and be done with it?

"Very mature . . ."

"Girls, please stop bickering; you're smudging the atmosphere," Joan pleaded.

Pushing her chair back, Scarlett stood up and opened the back door. Pulling a cigarette from a packet, she lit it and inhaled deeply, before blowing the smoke outside.

"Are you ever going to quit?" asked Wednesday, wrinkling her nose.

"Reformed smokers are the worst. You used to be just like me, remember? And they do say, once a smoker, always a smoker."

"Give it a rest, I feel much healthier since quitting. You should try it sometime," Wednesday interjected.

"Girls, what's happened to you?" Oliver asked with a quiet voice.

"She's got less patient since quitting, and she really needs a man," Scarlett snapped back.

"That's your domain; my career fulfils me adequately. You're just bitter over Lennox ending things."

"I wondered when you'd bring him up. You're resentful he went out with me; that he *chose* me."

"Enough," Oliver shouted. "Don't let a man get in the way of your relationship."

Scarlett crushed the tab end underfoot before grabbing her coat from the hook by the door. "I'll skip dessert if you don't mind." She blew kisses to her parents before disappearing into the grey night.

"It's me," Megan Hart said down the receiver.

"I wondered when I'd hear from you," replied Carl, in a hushed tone.

"Do you have the money?"

"I have some of it; I couldn't get it all."

Megan sighed. "I'll take what you have for now. Let's meet by The Corn Exchange at lunchtime."

"It might be difficult . . ."

"I don't care, make it." She rang off sharply.

"Who was that?" Tamara asked from the bedroom doorway.

"Just a work colleague, I'm needed to drop in at the hospital on my way to the clinic."

"Really? Meeting a charming doctor, per chance?"

He rolled his eyes before putting on his shoes. Tamara continued watching him, studying his every move as though she would never see him again.

"You're not doing anything nefarious, are you?" she asked.

"Like what?"

"Like meeting someone behind my back."

Carl laughed curtly. "As if I'd get the chance to do that with you skulking around me all the time. Perhaps you should start a personal daily diary again, you know it helps."

"Don't treat me like a bloody patient; I'm sanity personified."

"Then monitor the undercurrent of your paranoia before it consumes our relationship."

Carl arrived ten minutes early at The Corn Exchange. The imposing yellow and red brick building made him feel infinitesimally small.

Pacing back and forth, he zigzagged around people jostling for space on the pavement, until finally he spied Megan.

"Not here," she said, "we don't want it to look like a drug exchange." She threaded her arm through his, and led him away from the building.

Carl's arm stiffened at her touch, but he allowed himself to be guided by her to end the rendezvous as swiftly as possible.

"Shall we get a coffee?" she asked as they passed a café.

"Stop dragging this out. Just take the money and go; I have to get to back to work."

"When will you have the rest of the money?"

"I need a few more weeks; it's not that easy."

"Life isn't easy when you make mistakes along the way."

"It isn't easy when people who should be trusted turn out to be the vilest of villains," he answered dryly before handing her the envelope.

She stuffed it into her handbag before squeezing his arm. "Remember to be a good boy from now on," she winked as she walked away.

Carl returned to the clinic wondering how he was going to finally pay her off, fearing she may never stop asking for money.

Slumping back in the chair, Wednesday closed her eyes, letting the characters parade before her; trying to see them from another angle. Picking up her phone, she called Lennox and said they were going to visit Eileen Potter.

"Would it be possible to see your flat?" Wednesday asked Eileen as they stepped inside the hotel.

She led the pair up two flights of stairs, and into her flat under the eaves. A kitchenette sat in one corner of the room, with a tiny round table and two chairs neatly tucked underneath. The rest of the room housed an oversized sofa and armchair, positioned facing a wall-mounted large-screen TV.

Wednesday wandered over to the window and peered out.

"You have a good view of your garden. I don't suppose you remember anything different about that day, now a few days has elapsed."

"I don't spend my time gazing at the view; I know it too well."

"You can't hear the traffic from up here," Lennox declared.

Eileen shook her head. "So it goes without saying, I didn't hear the murder."

"You might have heard something else that doesn't appear connected to the crime. How about sitting down and closing your eyes, walk yourself through that evening," Lennox suggested, looking at Wednesday.

Eileen reluctantly did as requested, then Wednesday took over.

"I heard arguing in the hotel earlier in the evening. I recognised the dead man's voice, but I couldn't hear the other one properly."

"Male or female?"

"I don't know," she snapped.

"What happened after?"

"A door slammed, then silence."

"Did you leave your flat that evening?"

"I never go downstairs after the evening meal; I don't want to risk bumping into a guest, they always have demands."

"Fair enough. Were you disturbed during the night, perhaps?"

Eileen re-closed her eyes. "I did wake up at one point, but it was more to do with indigestion than an outside noise."

The argument was new information for the detectives, and the only people who could perhaps enlighten them was Carl Trott or Stella Hibit. Wednesday itched to leave the vertiginous flat and question them with the new evidence.

Chapter 13

Ever since her bitter divorce over a year ago, Stella's flat was tinged by the fusty smell of cats, which was barely masked by the lavender plug-in air freshener.

"Some new information has come to light about the victim, and we wondered if you could help us?" Wednesday asked, cringing at having to sit on a hairy sofa. "Someone was heard arguing with the victim late Saturday evening, and we wondered whether you knew anything about it?"

"That could be any member of the group; most of them despised him. He was an arrogant man."

"Jack Turner especially didn't like him."

"That's no surprise seeing as he fancied Isobel. He would have done anything to make her happy, given the opportunity."

"How do you know he was attracted to her?"

"I'm an observer of human behaviour and body language; everything about him was drawn to her."

"So he could have argued with the victim."

"As I've said, anyone could have. If the argument was overheard, how come you don't know whether it was a male or female he was having the argument with?"

"The person couldn't hear the other voice."

"Maybe a softly-spoken woman then."

"Perhaps. Any thoughts on that, from your knowledge of the group?"

"Isobel wasn't above arguing with him still, especially over Holly. Michelle Turner was flirtatious, she liked you," she said, nodding at

Lennox, "so she could have propositioned him and ended up arguing with him when he turned her down."

"Did you ever argue with him?"

"That would have been unprofessional. No matter what I thought of him in private, professionally I had to remain neutral."

"What *were* your private thoughts?"

"That he was an intolerable arsehole, who's ruined Isobel's life and that of the seventeen-year-old, no doubt. It may take her a while to trust to love again. And poor little Holly is now without a father, and will grow up to learn what kind of man he truly was."

"Maybe Isobel will shield her from that side of him."

"That won't stop others from telling her. Anyway, she could find out about him on the internet when she's older. Her new-found knowledge will only make her feel sad, and that angers me."

"Your dislike seems quite intense."

"And from that you deduce I killed him."

"I didn't say that."

"But you thought it."

"I can't imagine what your motive would be?"

"To rid the world of another cheating, misogynistic, and arrogant man."

"So what stopped you acting on your negative emotions?"

"I have an inbuilt moral compass."

"Is that just because you're a facilitator?"

"No, everyone should have one, but obviously that's not the case, or else you'd be out of a job. But you're asking me my personal view, and I'm not a saint. I can still have bad thoughts."

Wednesday smiled lightly. "Are you keeping in touch with the rest of the group?"

"Actually, we've just invited them all back to the hotel next weekend; we're paying the hotel bill, and they're paying half our fees, to complete the process. Isobel isn't attending, of course."

"Do you think that's wise; we haven't caught the killer."

"We'll make sure no one remains alone. Besides, no one was hated as much as Richie Dover was, so hopefully we'll all be safe."

"Perhaps somewhere in the back of your mind, you suspect Isobel capable of committing the crime. You laboured the point about his misdemeanour being hard to reconcile with."

"I struggle to see her wounding him like that. But I'm only a facilitator, not a clairvoyant."

Leaving Stella with her cats, they returned to the car and headed off to see Carl Trott.

Carl initially looked thunderous on opening the door, but rapidly transformed his face with a radiant smile when he saw them.

"To what do I owe this pleasure?"

"Just a quick question about an overheard argument with the victim," replied Wednesday.

"My argument?"

"When did your argument take place?"

He looked around before inviting them in, taking them through a door into his office, which was laid out with a couch, armchair, and desk.

"We converted the garage for when I go into private practice," he said, waving his arm around the space.

"So, your argument," Wednesday reiterated.

"He was riling everyone with his talk of his sexual prowess, so I had a word with him in the garden, after the end of the sessions, about toning it down. He didn't agree with my request, and I hate to say it, an argument ensued. He demolished my boundaries so I succumbed to verbalising my irritation with him, which is why I chose not to say anything; I'm embarrassed, I suppose."

"Then what happened?"

"We parted company; I could tell he wasn't listening to me. He was a frustrating man."

Eileen Potter showed Scarlett into her private lounge and offered her a drink.

"I'll pass, thanks. Now, tell me how you came about running the first divorce hotel weekend in the country."

"They offered me business at a good rate during a recession; it's a quiet period in the year. Mind you, I wish I hadn't bothered now, what with all this fuss."

"It's put your hotel on the ghoul map, though. What impression did the couples give you, especially the victim and his wife?"

"He walked around like he was a celebrity, but I'd never heard of him; I like Radio 4. His wife was pretty enough, but she looked unhappy, and I'm not surprised after hearing about his philandering."

"What did you hear, specifically?"

"Well," Eileen began, leaning in and speaking in a theatrical whisper, "he slept with a seventeen-year-old girl he met at one of those dance clubs."

"Seventeen, in a nightclub," Scarlett reiterated, scribbling the words rapidly. "Do you know who she is, and what nightclub?"

"No." Eileen sat back in her chair, puffing out her cheeks.

"It would appear the killer was someone in the hotel at that time. Do you have a theory?"

"Well it's not me or my staff. I'd lay my money on it being a member of the group, probably his wife, seeing as his manhood was cut off."

Scarlett kept her eye on her notepad as she scrawled Eileen's gems down, desperate to get back to the office to start writing her article. Eileen watched on, racking her brain for other things to say to keep the reporter in her clutches.

"They're all coming back to finish what they started; I can't wait to see what happens this time."

Scarlett smiled broadly. "If anything occurs, or you think of or hear anything else, please do give me a call," Scarlett said, handing her a business card before bolting for the door.

The Davenport Hotel awaited the arrival of the first guests. A frisson of excitement rippled through Hugo and Eileen as they hovered in the reception area.

"Do you think someone will get murdered again?" he asked.

"You sound like you'd like it to happen."

"It was a rush; I was in demand everywhere I went, everyone wanted to ask me questions. I was like a god."

"You young people are so foolish. You mistake transient emotions for reality. Society's ruined because of you."

"Geez Mrs P, why the downer?"

"You wouldn't understand."

They were interrupted by the arrival of Carl, who threw them a smile that did not reach his eyes.

"We're all ready for you, Mr Trott," she said.

At that moment, Stella blustered in, her leather satchel slung across her body; the strap cutting between her two ample breasts.

"Anyone arrived yet?" she puffed.

Carl shook his head. "Perhaps they've all changed their minds; I wouldn't be surprised."

"I think curiosity and the need for closure may shepherd them our way. You'll see."

"What about Isobel's closure?"

"I think we should offer to meet with her together. I've popped in a couple of times already, but it feels a tad awkward on my own."

The door opened behind them, and in walked Vincent and Sandra Vine, bringing with them a gust of wind, and a torrent of verbal abuse.

"If you'd done something other than raise our four kids, we may have had a future together. As it is, we've got fuck-all in common."

"Oh that's it, lower the tone with your foul mouth."

"Sandra, Vincent, good to see you again," Carl said quickly, stepping towards them.

"Can't say the same. If we don't come away with the paperwork this time, I'm going to the newspapers about this charade."

"No need to worry," interjected Stella. "We made a good start last time so we'll definitely get finished this time."

"Don't mind him," Sandra said, "he's been in a foul mood all morning."

"Perhaps you can share in the group session later," Stella suggested to him.

"*Marvellous*," he muttered.

Eileen handed out their keys, and Hugo carried Sandra's case upstairs, whilst Vincent mooched up behind them.

The rest of the group arrived, putting their trappings in their allotted rooms before descending to the lounge, where Carl and Stella awaited them. As Megan Hart entered the room, she let a smile drift across her lips as she locked eyes with Carl. He looked away swiftly.

"Welcome one and all," Carl began, "to the Parting Ways weekend part two; which should run smoothly this time, terminating your marriages in the peaceful manner you all seek."

"As long as the weekend is peaceful and I'm unhooked from him, then I'll be delighted," Michelle sniped.

"There won't be much peace with you and your bitter mouth constantly opening," Jack batted back.

"Well, I for one feel better in the presence of a calm and capable man," Michelle said, turning towards Carl.

Putting two fingers in her mouth, Sandra pretended to gag, making Jack smile broadly. Michelle was blind to the mockery, making it even sweeter in his eyes.

Stella swiftly took the group in hand, reminding them of the ground rules they had compiled in the last meeting; aware several rules had already been broken.

The group sat in a circle, with Carl and Stella sitting at each pole position.

"Who wants to go first?" she asked, eagerly sitting forward in her chair.

Washing her hands in the sink, Wednesday caught sight of her face. Her cheeks were beginning to fill out, and the hint of a bulge was introducing itself to her chin. Smoking had been replaced by snacking, and it had to stop.

Heading back to her office, she was pursued by Arlow, who was brandishing a piece of paper.

"Got a call from Hugo Frost saying someone's been taken seriously ill at The Davenport Hotel. He thought you'd like to know." Handing her the note, she glanced at it before announcing to Lennox that he was driving.

Chapter 14

Hugo's cheeks glowed like shiny gala apples on greeting the detectives. Everyone was gathered in the lounge, still wearing their night attire.

"Who's ill?" Wednesday asked, with a pronounced air of authority.

"Michelle Turner," Hugo replied eagerly.

"Where is she?"

"In the bedroom with the paramedics. Shall I take you?"

Wednesday nodded before the three of them strode upstairs.

Hugo hovered by the bedroom door as they entered without him, closing the door behind them.

The paramedics were working on Michelle Turner. Glancing up briefly, they acknowledged the pair.

"She needs to go to hospital now," one said.

"What can you tell us?" asked Wednesday, peering around him to see Michelle looking flushed and garbling nonsense.

"We're not sure exactly, but she's suffering with tachycardia, a sensitivity to light, and confusion. We need to go now."

The detectives stood to one side as the paramedics placed Michelle on a stretcher to carry her downstairs.

Everyone stopped talking as the detectives returned to the lounge.

"I don't understand how you come to be here, or the need for you?" Eileen frowned, having surfaced from her flat in fluffy slippers.

"Don't you find it strange that both times you all meet, something happens to one of you?" asked Wednesday, looking around at the group.

Eileen threw a fiery glance in Hugo's direction. "Mrs Turner's been taken ill, not murdered."

"We're not saying a crime's been committed, but it is suspicious, don't you think? Does your wife suffer with a heart condition?" she asked, turning to Jack.

"She's a healthy beast; no heart problems."

"How did this come about?"

"We women were getting ready to go upstairs; leaving the men to their misogynistic mutterings. When Michelle stood up and started staggering around, and slurring her words," said Megan, "I wondered whether she was diabetic, but Jack said not."

"She drank too much, I don't know why we're all fussing," Sandra chipped in.

"You've no compassion for her, you always thought she was stupid. Typical cold-hearted you," Vincent retorted.

Wednesday held out her hands to silence the pair.

"*Okay*, so was she drinking excessively?"

"No more than anyone else," said Hugo. "She only had three gin and tonics."

"And you served them all?"

Hugo nodded. The rest of the group stared intently at one another, allowing fear to slowly seep into their minds.

"You suspect foul play, otherwise you wouldn't be here," Megan whispered, pressing the palms of her hands together.

"We're just being cautious," Wednesday replied.

"When the press get to hear of this, our new business venture will be ruined," Stella moaned.

"That's not a very caring attitude," Jack snapped.

"There's a lot of negative vibes in the room. Let's all take a breather," Carl intercepted, putting his hand on Stella's arm, which she swiftly pulled away.

"Had Michelle eaten anything?" queried Wednesday.

"No, they were just having drinks," Eileen Potter said sharply. "I suppose the hotel will somehow be blamed for this." She pulled her cardigan tightly around her, bunching up her breasts.

"We don't know what's wrong with her. We'll know more after visiting the hospital, which is where we'll go now. We may need to see you all again afterwards." Wednesday said, sweeping the room with a stare.

They left the group to bicker amongst themselves as they headed for the hospital.

Michelle Turner had been transferred to the Intensive Care Unit by the time they arrived. A nurse asked them to wait for a doctor to update them.

Fifteen minutes later, a doctor, looking young enough to be Wednesday's son, approached them. "We've had a devil-of-a-time working this one out," he laughed, only stopping short on seeing Wednesday's expression.

"Her blood results ruled out excessive alcohol or a stroke, which is good news in itself. However, we are lucky enough to have a doctor-on-call with an interest in natural poisons. He needs further tests to back up his theory, but he suspects deadly nightshade to be the culprit."

"Really?" queried Wednesday. "Isn't that difficult to come by these days?"

"Apparently it grows sparingly in twenty-eight counties in the UK, but he could tell you in more detail."

"We'll await the diagnosis first. Can we talk to her yet?"

"She's too confused currently. Tomorrow may be better."

They strolled back to the car, disappointed by the stalemate.

"Deadly nightshade's an old-fashioned poison," Lennox said, sliding into the car.

"I suppose so, but it's free, no lingering fingerprints to be found, and less risky than purchasing a weapon."

"I wouldn't even know what it looks like."

"There are no secrets with the internet, these days."

"Are we looking at two criminals; the crimes are so different?"

"Poisoning does tend to be favoured by women. However, nothing can be ruled out at this moment in time. For now, I want to treat the two crimes individually, but with a helicopter-mind spanning both incidents."

"If Michelle dies, it means the house and dog are automatically yours, I presume," Vincent whispered to Jack as they eyed the buffet spread out before them.

"I suppose that means you and everyone else believes I harmed her in some way."

"We don't know what's happened, but yes, I suppose that does put you in the spotlight."

"Great, I can surely expect another visit from the police."

"Well it is rather suspicious, isn't it? First Richie dies, and then Michelle is taken mysteriously ill."

"What do you want me to say?"

"I suppose the truth is too much to ask for. I imagine the doctors will be running a series of tests; they'll find out soon enough what's wrong with her."

Jack took a large swig of beer from the bottle before moving away from the food. Vincent watched him order another bottle before disappearing into the garden.

Lennox studied the nurses as they strolled along the corridor whilst he waited for Wednesday to make contact with the doctor.

"He's not answering his bleep, and the nurse can't give me the info we need. Typical," she muttered, flopping down onto the seat next to him. "Means you can spend longer ogling them though."

"No harm in looking, I am single."

"Never for long."

Their musings were interrupted by the piercing sound of an alarm, followed by a flurry of activity. They watched as a crash-cart rushed past them and into a room.

"Is that Turner's room?" Lennox asked, standing up.

"I believe so," she replied, also standing and taking a few paces towards the room, only to be waved back by an officious nurse.

They stood motionless as the scene reached its crescendo with voices calling out, and more staff entering the room, before resuming a heavy calmness. A red-faced doctor approached them, sweat glistening on his brow.

"I'm sorry to inform you, Michelle Turner died a few minutes ago," he said shakily.

"What happened?" Wednesday asked.

"We struggled to regulate her tachycardia, and she suffered a massive coronary. We were unable to revive her."

The case was now a murder enquiry, placing it squarely alongside the Dover case, with the hotel and the occupants as the common denominators.

When Jack Turner opened his front door, the drawn expression on his sallow face indicated he had already learnt of Michelle's death.

"You're quick to get here, I've only just heard the news."

"We were waiting to talk to your wife when she passed away. Very sorry," replied Wednesday.

"For you perhaps, as you didn't get the chance to speak with her."

"Can we come in?"

Stepping back and picking up the dog, he ushered them in, closing the door quietly behind him.

The lounge was dominated by a plasma TV mounted above the

fireplace, housing only an electric real-fire-looking unit. A glass showcase housing golf trophies stood in one corner of the room, and an elaborate sound system stood in another. The air was tainted with the dusty smell of potpourri, ill-disguising the smell of dog, placed as offerings in glass bowls dotted around the room.

There was a plethora of photographs of the springer spaniel who had now jumped up on the sofa next to Wednesday. There were no photographs of the couple.

"I can't remember what the doctor said she died of."

"Cardiac arrest."

"She didn't have a heart problem, I don't understand."

"Hopefully the autopsy will reveal more." The dog snuggled into Wednesday's thigh.

"You suspect she was murdered, don't you? Otherwise why would you be here?"

"It's not a certainty as yet; we're following an enquiry-line presently."

Jack hunched forward, clasping his knees with both hands. His tongue moistening his parched lips.

"Had you and Michelle managed to resolve your divorce issues? I remember you were both disagreeing over the house and the custody of your dog," she continued, feeling the hot breath of the dog on her hand.

"The counselling sessions had almost made us agree to sell the house and split the money, but as for Jasper," he said, looking at the dog, "neither of us were prepared to give him up."

"Were you discussing shared custody?" Lennox asked, shuddering at the memories.

"We knew Jasper would feel too unsettled; he had to have one home. Besides, we didn't want to keep meeting up to hand him over; a clean cut was needed."

"So what were you going to do?" Wednesday persisted.

Jack sighed, rubbing the top of his head with the palm of his hand.

"My solicitor was going to use the fact that she was out of the house seven hours a day, whereas I work from home in between visiting properties, so Jasper would hardly ever be on his own. I was going to win that way."

Wednesday perused the room, her eyes drawn to the framed photographs of stately homes and gardens.

"They're some of the places I've sold," he said proudly. "I only deal with high-end properties."

"I won't be coming to your agency then," Lennox quipped.

Wednesday shot him a glance. "Did you leave the hotel at any time?"

"No, but Paul did to eat at that veggie restaurant."

"Apart from Paul, were you all together all of the time?"

"I think so. Could we do this another time? I really must get on and phone the family."

Rising from her seat, Wednesday nodded. The dog grumbled at being disturbed, before jumping off the sofa and launching himself straight onto Jack's lap.

"You'll keep me informed of how you're doing, won't you?" he said, stroking Jasper along his spine.

They both climbed into the car before Wednesday turned on the ignition.

"I wasn't sure how he'd be today. I mean, they were in the process of divorcing. I wasn't sure if he'd be upset or not," Lennox said, toying with the packet of cigarettes in his pocket.

"His main concern was the dog, which he now owns outright. He didn't feel the need to pretend with us."

They drove the rest of the way in silence, each pondering the intricacies of the case.

Isobel answered the door to find Jack standing before her. She looked down at the baggy grey joggers she was wearing and mumbled an embarrassed apology, running her fingers through her hair.

"I need to see you," he said, stepping inside.

Chapter 15

"If you'd told me you were coming, I'd have made myself look more presentable," Isobel said, as Jack sat on the sofa.

"That matters not," he replied, patting the space next to him.

She obliged meekly, sitting with the base of her spine pressed into the arm rest, so she was facing him. He proceeded in telling her the news of Michelle's death, which felt like a blow to her stomach, winding her and causing her to gasp for breath. He took her hand in his.

"Don't be upset, I'm fine."

"It's the shock of another death so close to Richie's. She never mentioned she was ill."

"She wasn't. The police are looking into her death; they were with me earlier."

"They suspect you murdered her?" she whispered, noticing the layer of sweat between their clasped hands.

"It's par for the course; I'm sure they suspected you of Richie's death at first."

She nodded before gently teasing her hand out of his grip. "Let me put the kettle on and throw on some jeans. I'll be back shortly."

He watched her creep out of the room, his eyes lingering on the arch of her back.

Isobel stared at her reflection as she hoisted up a pair of skinny jeans and fastened them. She decided to keep her face free from make-up, but spritzed some perfume around her neck. The bed caught her eye, sending a ripple across her shoulders. She swapped her slippers for loafers before descending downstairs to find Jack studying a photo of her on the mantelpiece.

"You look melancholic in this," he said, without turning around.

"I'd just discovered another of Richie's affairs, but I hadn't as yet told him I knew. He said I looked sexy in the photo; showed how little he knew me."

"Oh I don't know; I think he was right, personally." Turning around, he smiled at her, before moving towards her.

Edmond was deep in conversation with Alex when Wednesday arrived.

"Ah, just the person," beamed Alex. "The results are through for Michelle Turner. It's confirmed as atropa belladonna poisoning; deadly nightshade."

"Did you know that Venetian women once used it in eye drops to dilate their pupils, making them appear more seductive?" chipped in Edmond.

Wednesday listened as Edmond moved on to telling her the symptoms of the poisoning, such as blurred vision, sensitivity to light, loss of balance, slurred speech, staggering, and tachycardia.

"So she presented as drunk, explaining why people didn't rush to help her instantly," she added.

"Indeed. All parts of the plant are poisonous, but especially the berries," confirmed Alex.

"Tell me more."

"It does grow in the UK, but sparingly. It's a large, upright, herbaceous perennial, with faintly scented purple flowers, and glossy-black berries which are apparently sweet. It mostly grows in wastelands, quarries, and near old ruins."

"Is there an antidote?"

"Physostigmine and pilocarpine are available, but need to be given early on. But nothing's guaranteed," Edmond stated.

"How would someone ingest it?"

"You can make a pie with the sweet berries; it's been used in past murders. The berry juice can be hidden in an alcoholic drink; there's no bitterness to mask."

"This was clearly a deliberate act, making this another murder of a member of the group. I'll go back to the hotel with Lennox and see who's replaced Tim Binder as the chef."

Rain lashed down onto the windscreen as Wednesday drove to the hotel. Lennox shoved his mobile back in his pocket.

"No answer from the hotel?" Wednesday said, irritated by the weather and lack of response. "I wonder if we'll find it closed?"

"Makes her vulnerable to losing passing trade. I would have thought that Frost guy would at least be on reception."

The windscreen wipers sloshed water onto the side windows, before it splayed out like the far-reaching fingers of palm leaves, clinging desperately to the glass until the momentum spun the droplets off.

"How's Joan?"

"Stable, thanks. She still asks after you."

"Does she still refer to me as your boyfriend?"

Wednesday laughed. "Periodically."

"Perhaps we should follow her lead."

Wednesday frowned sharply before swerving into a parking space outside the hotel, and yanking on the handbrake.

They rang the doorbell and waited for someone to answer. Stepping back, Wednesday looked up, sheltering her eyes from the rain, to see if there was any movement at the windows.

"Boss," Lennox called as Hugo opened the front door.

They followed him inside, brushing the raindrops from their coats.

"Is Mrs Potter available?" she asked.

"She's been in her flat all morning."

"Has she replaced Tim Binder?"

"You're looking at him," he grinned. "I'm the cook, barman, and waiter, for now. She said she couldn't be bothered to interview anyone. She's been down with all the things going on right now."

"You prepared the drinks for everyone when Michelle Turner was taken ill, correct?"

"Mrs P was right; she said you'd blame us."

"We're seeking the answer to how the victim was poisoned."

"Poisoned," he exclaimed. "I never did that." His ears turned puce.

"Did anyone else have access to making the drinks behind the bar?"

He rolled his eyes, finally resting on the ceiling. "Not that I remember, which means you think I did it." His wide eyes stared at her.

"There were no other fingerprints on the glasses except for yours and the recipient of the drink. You'd better go and advise Mrs Potter that we're coming to search the premises, and we'll be checking out your home too."

Lennox phoned the station as Hugo jogged up to Eileen's flat. Wednesday smiled wryly at the sound of feet pounding down the stairs.

"It's an outrage," screamed Eileen. "We're the innocent party here; it's that group you need to scrutinise. I rue the day I ever agreed to house that lot." She displayed a head tremor which made wisps of hair flutter around her scalp like mosquitos.

"We'll be checking out their rooms too, so could you call everyone down?" Wednesday requested.

"They're already down, some sort of group therapy in the guest lounge," she replied, jerking her head forcefully in the direction of a closed door.

Arlow and Damlish arrived at the hotel with the warrant and a couple of extra officers to carry out the search. Another two officers were on their way to Hugo's mother's house to search his bedroom.

"She'll go nuts," he said, grabbing his mobile and dashing to the kitchen, where two officers were already searching through the cupboards.

Wednesday and Lennox entered the guest lounge to advise them all of the plan.

"You can't just barge in here," Carl snapped.

Stella stood up, nodding in agreement.

"A second murder within this group would say otherwise. We'd like you all to remain in here until we've finished our search of the entire premises, including your rooms."

Rumbling paroxysms echoed around the room, as the shockwave bounced from wall to wall.

"It looked like a stroke. You said it was a stroke," Sandra hissed accusingly to Paul and Megan.

"We're nurses, yes, but we can't always see the answers without running a few tests. What did she die of exactly?" he asked, turning to Wednesday.

"She was poisoned. You will all be interviewed shortly, but for now, remain in here until we call you. We'll use your office, Mrs Potter."

Arlow and Damlish were busy searching the kitchen, so Wednesday and Lennox snapped on gloves and headed for the bar in the dining room.

"You don't think we'll find anything, do you?" asked Lennox, removing bottles from the shelves.

"I think all the poison was used in one go, but every criminal makes mistakes along the way; I'm just hoping this is where they've tripped up."

"If it's Hugo Frost, he may not have been so careful in his own home. Perhaps the guys will come up trumps there."

"I'm not sure what his motive would be."

"Perhaps he has a secret the victims discovered, so they had to go."

"But the death of Richie would have been a warning to Michelle; she would have come to us, surely?"

"Not unless it took her a few days to work it out, by which time it was too late."

Turning her back to him, Wednesday began searching the drawers underneath the bar, preferring to listen to her own mind chatter.

Out of the corner of her eye, a figure hovered in the doorway. Looking up, the figure retreated. Wednesday hailed Lennox's attention by squeezing his arm and motioning him to go out the first door whilst she took the door leading to the kitchen.

Like the swift blades of scissors, the pair cornered Hugo in the walk-in pantry by the kitchen entrance. His wide eyes darted between the pair; his nostrils flaring as they spluttered with rapid air flow.

"Calm down," ordered Lennox, stretching out his arm in an attempt to placate him.

"I've done nothing wrong; I didn't know," he said in an adolescent-like pitch.

"You didn't know what?" Wednesday quizzed.

He hesitated for a few calming moments before his breathing began steadying, and a cocky smirk graced his face. "I know nothing about any of these crimes. You've got nothing on me, have you?" he said, looking reassured.

"Why were you skulking in the doorway?" pressed Lennox, not budging from his position.

"I was hoping to pick up a few juicy facts to tell my mates."

"Cocky sod," muttered Lennox.

"You're wasting time on me when a murderer is getting away with it right under your noses."

Lennox's jaw muscles twitched as his eyes narrowed on the boy. "If we later find you've hidden facts pertaining to this case, we'll haul your butt into a cell, where your smug attitude will dissolve in the presence of truly dangerous men."

"You don't scare me, old man."

Wednesday reacted to the testosterone-filled air by standing between the pair. "Go back to the others and stay there until further notice," she instructed Hugo, before glaring at Lennox then swiftly turning away.

A red-faced officer was trapped against the wall, with Ray Frost's hand around his neck, and the tip of a knife pressing into him just below his left ear. The other officer stood in the doorway, speaking calmly.

"We do have a warrant, sir. Let my colleague go, and we can talk about this."

"I'm not talking to you lot. If my fucking son's done something stupid, then deal with him, don't invade my home," he spat.

"Your son resides here; we have to search where *he* lives."

The officer spluttered as Ray's grip tightened.

"I'm warning you, touch anything and your mate's dead."

Pressing the speed-dial button on the mobile in his pocket, the officer stepped back a pace. "You're only making the situation worse. Let my colleague go and put the knife down."

Wednesday answered her mobile.

"Officer in trouble at the Frost household. Weapon involved."

She bellowed to Lennox, rushing to her car.

Chapter 16

Lennox gripped the dashboard as Wednesday screeched around the corner, almost clipping the curb. Pulling in front on the house, she had barely switched the engine off before opening the door.

They both cantered up to the house, finding the front door open. On entering, PC Barnes turned around, as did Ray Frost.

"What the fuck do you want?" Ray yelled, pushing the tip of the blade further into Thomas's flesh. A pinprick of blood surfaced.

"I wouldn't do that if I were you," Wednesday said quietly. "You're already in a bad situation; you don't want to make it worse."

"I don't want you lot snooping around; you'll plant evidence and have me away before I can take another breath."

"We're here about your son, not you. Why would we be interested in you?"

"Because I have form. Why are you interested in Hugo? He's a daft bugger, but he's no criminal, he's done better than me."

"Then let us prove it. Let us look around and see for ourselves. You're impeding our investigation."

A fraction of the tension in Ray's hand released, allowing PC Thomas to push his wrist away as PC Barnes lunged towards his shoulder. The three of them scuffled around until Ray's right arm was yanked up behind his back. He yelled out with pain as he was brought to his knees. Barnes whipped out a pair of handcuffs and fastened his wrists securely.

"Take him away," ordered Wednesday before mounting the stairs, two-by-two, followed by Lennox.

The first bedroom clearly belonged to the parents, with the salmon-coloured candlewick bedspread and pile of fishing magazines on one bedside table, and well-thumbed romantic novels on the other.

They moved to the next room which was Hugo's; the unmade bed and dirty items of clothing strewn across the floor gave it away. Wednesday headed for the wardrobe as Lennox bent down to check under the bed.

He found a small pile of pornographic magazines, a box of paraphernalia for smoking cannabis, some dusty odd socks, and a tin containing seven hundred pounds in notes. He alerted Wednesday.

"Bag it, we'll ask him about it at the station. Let's see if we can find anything else," she said, continuing to riffle through a set of drawers.

Forty minutes later, the pair assembled in the kitchen.

"We haven't found much," Wednesday said, leaning against the worktop.

"Perhaps the money will lead us to something more tangible."

Wednesday shrugged, throwing the bagged tin into her bag.

"Let's get back. I'll give this to Alex to process, and this," she said holding up a laptop, "to see what his research history brings up."

"I hear Alex is all loved-up," Lennox said, watching her in his peripheral vision. "How do you feel about that?"

"How do you want me to feel? Distraught, gutted, pining? I wish him all the best and I hope it works out for him."

"That's big of you," he smiled.

"Nothing of the sort, we were never an item." Picking up her bag, she headed for the door.

Hugo Frost slumped into the chair in the interview room, crossing his arms over his chest, and jutting out his jaw.

"Where's this money from?" asked Wednesday, thrusting the evidence bag across the table.

"Savings."

"Come on, from your hotel job? I doubt it. What else are you doing on the side?"

"Nothing."

"I bet Mrs Potter would be interested in where you got it from."

He scowled at them. "It's none of her business, or yours."

"We have to guess it's from a nefarious source, otherwise you'd tell us."

He shifted in his seat, as though sitting on an army of red ants. "I do odd jobs for people; putting up shelves and such-like."

"Do you declare it?"

He shook his head, his chin dipping towards his chest.

"We'll need a list of the people you worked for, to corroborate your story." She shoved a pen and pad across to him.

"I can't remember their names and addresses; I'll need to go home for that."

"I thought that would be your answer. Let's cut the crap, where's the money really come from?"

"I sell stuff on the side; not drugs, you understand."

"Then what?" Wednesday was beginning to lose her patience.

"Alcohol. I sell bottles from the hotel. Mrs P is so dense she doesn't notice what I order."

"Who do you sell them to?"

"Friends, family, neighbours. I suppose you're going to tell her now."

"She'll be made aware of the fact."

"She'll probably sack me."

"That's as maybe. The truth might help you with us, however."

"That is the truth; I've nothing more to say." He slumped further down in the chair, until his feet were touching Lennox's.

Lennox growled making him spring back up.

"If we find you've hidden facts pertinent to the case, you'll be charged alongside the theft," Wednesday warned.

Hugo's face turned flaxen. His eyes darted around the room. "Look, I let someone in that night, but not to commit murder."

"Who and why?"

"Damien Philpot. He said he had a score to settle with one of the guests."

"And you let him in?"

"He only wanted to punch the guy a few times, that's all, I swear."

"Which guy?"

"The guy who was murdered."

Chapter 17

The path up to the Philpot's house was crazy-paved in terracotta and beige slabs, with an assortment of cracked and chipped pots dotted about. A plastic bag full of empty bottles lay discarded in front of the wheelie bin, and the front gate had rusted off its hinges and lay propped up against the low wall.

The doorbell activated the yapping of a dog, followed by shouts for it to cease. As the door opened, a rat-like Yorkshire terrier shot out and encircled their ankles excitedly.

"DI Wednesday and DS Lennox. Is Damien home?"

"No. He's probably down the snooker club. What do you want him for?"

"May we come in for a brief chat?"

They found themselves in a long, narrow lounge diner, decorated with coffee-coloured walls and a cream ceiling. A gaudy gilt lamp stood on a sideboard, and a teak coffee table stood in front of a dilapidated sofa, covered with dog hair. A young girl sat cross-legged on the floor with open arms to greet the dog.

"What's the silly sod done now?" Karen said, with her hands on her fleshy hips.

"It's to do with the murder at The Davenport Hotel." Wednesday replied.

"I saw it on the news. He didn't do it did he?"

"Mum," screeched the girl, the first interaction she had given since their arrival.

"What do you know about it?" Wednesday asked the sullen-looking girl.

"All I know is the love of my life is dead, and I'll never be the same again. He was the one," she sobbed.

Her mother turned to her. "What are you on about, Chanel? You're not talking about that dead bloke, are you?" she said sharply.

Chanel let out a louder sob before dashing upstairs.

"Come back here, girl, and explain yourself."

A door upstairs slammed loudly, muffling the sounds of distress.

"Mrs Philpot, could we take a seat and have a chat?" Wednesday asked calmly.

The woman's shoulders sagged as she flopped into an armchair. The detectives sat on the sofa, sinking further down than they had anticipated.

"You seem to know more about what's going on here," she muttered. "Fill me in, would you." Her eyes narrowed, staring at Wednesday.

"It appears your daughter met the deceased at a nightclub, and had a brief relationship with him. Your son found out, and wanted to teach him a lesson."

"By killing him?"

"That's what we're trying to get to ascertain. I'd like to speak to Chanel and see what she has to say. You can sit in with us if that's what she wants."

"I think she'll talk more truthfully if I'm not in the room." Her hand shook as she pointed upstairs.

Leaving the bewildered mother, they headed upstairs. Chanel's bedroom door was decorated with a large poster of a boy band, belying her protestations of being mature enough to love an older man.

Her voice cracked as she accepted their request to enter.

"Tell us about how you and Richie met?"

Chanel sat up on her bed, tipping her head back to reminisce.

"I'd been to the Roxy nightclub a couple of times, and the DJ always caught my eye, 'cause he used to stare and me and get me up with him on stage to ask what music I wanted. He made me feel special; he said I wasn't like all the other girls." She drifted off into a reverie before giving Lennox fleeting eye contact.

"In what way were you different?" coaxed Wednesday.

"He said I was mature and sophisticated, and I didn't dress like a tart."

"So where did you two go to meet up?"

"Sometimes he'd take me to a Premier Inn after the club closed, and sometimes he'd pick me up at the end of my road. When he wasn't working, we'd go to different hotels and stay in a room for a couple of hours; he said we couldn't go to restaurants where he'd be recognised, as he was famous 'cause of his radio show."

Lennox coughed to hide his derogatory laugh. Wednesday threw him a heated glance.

"What did you do when you were together?"

Chanel pressed her hands together, looking at Wednesday with confusion in her eyes.

"We made love, of course. He said I was the most beautiful woman he'd ever been with, and I made him happy. *She* didn't make him happy but she didn't want him to find happiness with someone else. She killed him for that reason."

"Who did?"

"His wife, of course."

"How did your brother find out about you two?"

"That stupid Hugo. He heard Richie talking about me, and he told Damien. I told him it was none of his business. He told me Richie was bragging about shagging a seventeen-year-old. He said it wasn't love, that I was one of many."

"How did that make you feel?"

"I knew he was wrong, and I told him so. Richie loved me; he was going to leave his wife and set up home with me."

"Did Damien threaten Richie?"

"He said nothing to me about it, and I don't believe he'd kill him. He talks big, but he's a pussycat."

"Had Richie told his wife he was leaving her?"

"Yes, he said they had a blazing row and that was why she wanted a speedy divorce with a big payoff."

"Had you met their daughter?"

"I'd seen photos of her. He said I'd make a better mother than *her*."

"Had you made any plans about where you were going to live?"

"He talked about getting a flat overlooking the river. There was a park nearby where I could've taken Holly."

"If you know about your brother's involvement in Richie's death, then you must say so now."

"I don't, and I wouldn't be talking to him if I thought he'd done it." A lone tear trickled down her cheek, which she quickly wiped away with the back of her hand.

"Thank you for your time. Perhaps you should talk to your mother about all of this."

The girl nodded before flopping back down on the bed and screwing her eyes shut.

Lennox slid into the driver's seat and slammed the door.

"Everything all right?" she asked.

"I wish Lucy and I had only had dogs instead of children. Teenagers suck the very soul out of life itself."

Crunching the gears, he set the car in motion.

"I thought things had settled down now Lucy and Brian are married."

"Lucy's pregnant, and the boys are freaking out, according to Alfie. Archie's been released, but he's not responding well to their news."

"Is this where you patch-up your relationship with your sons, perhaps?"

"I thought that too, but Archie's still refusing to see me; and now he's riddled with anger towards Lucy."

"The poor kid's got nowhere to turn. How's Lucy coping with it all?"

"Her rage towards me is more intense and sustained."

"This isn't your fault."

"Try telling her that."

Lennox swung into a parking space in the pub car park, pulling on the handbrake with overzealous vigour.

They entered the pub, heading straight for the pool room after quickly scanning for Damien Philpot.

The clacking sound of cue balls hitting one another informed them that a game was underway. They strolled in, mindful of not scaring Damien away, and their calmness paid off as they saw him resting belly-down along the table, preparing to take a shot. His focus never wavered as he drew back the cue and struck the ball firmly.

Wednesday strolled around the table in one direction, whilst Lennox took the other. Before he knew it, Damien was surrounded, although lacking in knowledge regarding their reasoning.

"We'd like you to come down to the station with us," commanded Wednesday, stepping closer.

"What about?" he asked, rubbing chalk on his cue.

"You wanting to settle a score with the victim, Richie Dover."

He paused, looking at her briefly before chucking the cue and chalk at her. Turning swiftly, he bolted straight into Lennox's arms. They tousled like novices learning to tango before Lennox managed to control him.

"All right, all right, I was there that night, but he was already dead when I got there," he spluttered.

"Nice story," Wednesday replied, "but too convenient."

"It's the truth, I'm telling you."

"Didn't stop you taking his watch though."

"Okay, that was a mistake, but . . ."

"Take us back to the beginning."

He told them how Hugo met them all at the pub, and regaled them with stories of the warring couples who had arrived at the hotel. He told them about this one guy who was bragging about sleeping with a seventeen-year-old.

"I was curious about that story, and asked Hugo to get more details, which he did when serving him drinks. It turned out he was the fucker who slept with my sister; she's been cut-up since he dumped her."

"So you went to punish him?"

"Yes, I went to punch his smug little face, only when I got there, somebody had got there before me."

"But you didn't alert anyone to your discovery."

"Of course not; I shouldn't have been there in the first place. I would have been your only suspect."

"You put yourself firmly in that position by *not* calling in your discovery."

His face crumpled into a mass of premature lines as the enormity of the situation dropped on him. Fear welled up in his eyes as he looked between the two detectives, his furred tongue moistening his dry lips.

"You'll have to come to the station, and we need your trainers too."

They arrived at his home, greeted once again by the yapping dog and stern-faced mother. She watched silently as they accompanied Damien to his room to collect his trainers.

Returning downstairs, Wednesday informed Mrs Philpot of their plans, asking her to accompany her son if they both so wished.

"I don't need her; I've done nothing wrong, you've got to believe me, Mum."

Her forehead erupted into a mass of creases before walking back to a bottle of gin sitting on the kitchen table.

"You've changed; I know you're up to something," Tamara said quietly.

"Not this again," groaned Carl. "I'm not in the mood."

"You're not in the mood for anything these days."

"Here we go again. Are you surprised I don't find you attractive in bed?"

"I knew you'd blame me for this. I've tried wearing sexy clothes, sexy underwear, and even role play. You're a hard man to please, Carl."

"It's your behaviour you need to change, not your appearance."

Dropping to the floor, she looked up at him with sad, Labrador-like eyes. "I love you, I need you. You can't leave me now."

"Then stop smothering me with your accusations of having affairs; it's tiresome."

"You seem to forget that's how we started. I'm no fool."

He moved away from her and disappeared towards the front door. She remained on the floor, holding back tears she was desperate to shed, but knew that they would only serve to flood any hope she had about remaining with Carl.

Alex Green tapped on Wednesday's office door, beaming as she looked up at him.

"I have the result from the hunting knife; but as we feared, any prints were wiped off."

"But it's definitely the murder weapon?"

"Affirmative."

"But nothing to link it to any of the suspects. That's disappointing."

"CSU didn't find any other fingerprints, other than the suspects' and the victim's, in the dining room or on the French doors leading to the garden."

"That would lead us to believe it was an inside job, not some random stranger."

"Anyway, I'll get back to start processing Damien Philpot's trainers. They've been cleaned, but that never removes all the evidence."

Wednesday watched him bound away, full of youthful enthusiasm, and found herself missing his attention. She seemed to remember

Lennox warning her it would happen. Shaking her head, she pulled a chocolate bar from her desk drawer and popped a large chunk into her mouth before walking over to Lennox's office.

"Let's go and see Isobel Dover now, whilst awaiting the results on the trainers; let Damien stew for a while."

On arriving at her house, they were surprised to find Jack Turner sitting in her kitchen. His face reddened on seeing them.

"Don't you ever warn people of your visits?" he asked.

"Sometimes," Wednesday smiled. "What brings you here?"

He glanced in Isobel's direction. "Just a friendly visit to check how she's doing, that's all."

"We'd like to talk with you in private," she said to Isobel.

It took Jack several seconds to catch on.

"I was going anyway. Give me a call, anytime," he said, leaning in hesitantly, then pulling back sharply before leaving.

"We've been speaking with the girl your husband had an affair with," Wednesday said.

"Huh, what did she have to say for herself?"

"Quite a lot. She mentioned you knew that Richie was leaving you for her."

Tipping her head back, Isobel laughed.

"What a gullible girl. He would have said those things just to get her into bed, and it worked."

"Why did he admit to this liaison?"

"A girlfriend of mine saw them together in the club. I confronted him, but he said it was nothing serious. To him, she was another body to roll around with to inflate his already huge ego. She's delusional if she believes he loved her. He only loved himself."

"He loved his daughter."

Isobel shrugged. "Fat lot that will do her now."

"Effectively, you have everything you want now he's dead."

"Good things come to those who wait, apparently," she smiled.

"Did you intend waiting, or did you conspire to move things on?"

Folding her arms, Isobel looked at Wednesday. "I won't waste my breath on answering that."

She got up and showed them out, closing the door firmly behind them.

Carl sat opposite Stella, his hands cupping a large mug of coffee.

"All the couples are now officially divorced," she said triumphantly. "We should congratulate ourselves for pulling it off."

He raised his mug in a mock salute.

"What's wrong with you? Thanks to all the free publicity after the murder, our Parting Ways course has attracted lots more people in need of our service. Surely you should be more jubilant."

"Sorry, it's just Tamara and I had a row before I came here. She's off on one of her paranoia episodes."

"If a woman had been murdered, I would have suspected her. She could have misconstrued a professional relationship for something else."

Carl almost choked on the mouthful of coffee. "You don't think her capable of murder, surely?"

"A woman with that amount of passion and distrust would be capable of anything, I imagine."

He sat back in the chair, expelling air, deflating his cheeks.

"Never mind, I'm just being foolish. Look, let's sift through these applicants, and see what we can organise. We'll probably get at least nine weekends out of this lot."

He smiled at her before picking up an application form to browse.

Wednesday's phone was ringing as she entered her office. It was Alex.

"I've matched Damien Philpot's trainers to the crime scene. Same sole print, plus there are flecks of Dover's blood on them."

He rang off, but instead of feeling elated, she felt low in mood. Placing Damien at the scene of the crime was one thing, but proving he did it was going to prove challenging, especially when she believed he was innocent. For now, his life would be put into the hands of the solicitor, until evidence could prove or disprove his guilt.

She and Lennox returned to the interview room to update Damien and his solicitor.

"I told you I was there and that's how the blood got on my trainers. He was already dead. He was; you've got to believe me."

The solicitor put his hand on Damien's arm.

"So far you can charge my client only with theft. The blood evidence isn't proof his guilt. I suggest he's released on bail whilst awaiting further information."

Wednesday did not believe he had committed the crime, so Damien was released a frailer looking boy than the one they brought in from the snooker club.

"Do you fancy coming over for dinner tonight? I've got some Cumberland sausage from the farmer's market, if you fancy?" Wednesday asked as they returned to the Incident Room.

"Compared to the microwave jacket potato and beans I had planned, that sounds perfect."

He watched her walking away, trying to calm his rapid heartbeat. He picked up his mobile and pressed speed dial.

"Hello Dad, I need some advice."

Wednesday answered the door wearing a pair of denim flares and a rock band t-shirt. Lennox was still wearing his suit. The air was plump with the aroma of sausage, herbs, and onions.

"Fancy a beer?" she asked, handing him a bottle without waiting for a response.

She saw him toying with his cigarette packet in his jacket pocket.

"You can smoke by the back door, I don't mind."

"I never thought you'd give up; I wish I had your will power."

"Perhaps when your personal life calms down a bit, you could give it a try."

"Maybe," he replied, drawing deep and blowing the smoke into the damp evening air. "You believe Damien Philpot's innocent, don't you?"

"I do, actually."

"He's got motive and we can place him at the scene. A jury would be hard-pressed not to convict him."

"I know, but there's something niggling me, and I can't see what it is. He doesn't seem capable of the offence somehow."

She got up and served the meal onto two plates before placing them on the table.

"Do you miss Scarlett living here?"

"I was considering asking her back, until I remembered all the annoying habits she has. The peace is lovely most of the time, but painful at others. How about you; are you getting used to living alone?"

"Not something I do out of choice."

"Is that why you still almost live at work?"

"It's absorbing, what's a man to do?"

"Get a girlfriend and a life."

"Hark at you. You're not exactly brimming over with an exciting personal life; unless you're planning on making a move on Hunter."

"Digby's too occupied with the impending divorce to start a new relationship, even if I were interested."

"What happened to you two after his birthday party?"

"Absolutely nothing."

Lennox sliced off a large chunk of sausage and put it in his mouth, leaving him no option but to saviour the taste and forget ribbing his boss, who clearly was not in the mood.

On the other side of Cambridge, Damien Philpot stood on a railway bridge, contemplating the charges against him. He took another swig of vodka and waited for numbness to rise up from his feet.

Chapter 18

"That's the last of my stuff," said Paul Hart, holding a box full of knick-knacks; remnants of his life with Megan.

"I can't believe it's come to this," she said, her voice tinged with regret.

"You're the one who changed. You see your career in monetary terms rather than seeing it as a way to give back to society."

"So you consider stitching up drunks' heads as more valuable than hoisting-up women's breasts, therefore boosting their confidence, do you?"

"But it doesn't stop there, does it? Once a woman starts surgically improving her looks, she's no longer satisfied with the decline into older-age. Suddenly, they're clones of their former selves, with bland personalities to match."

"And once a drunk has had his head stitched up, he goes off booze, does he? No, he continues down the same self-destructive path, to be periodically bailed out by people like you."

Paul stared at the woman who used to be his wife, and wondered whether she always had those values, but kept them deeply hidden.

"I don't know when you became so materialistic, but it's not endearing. And I don't know how suddenly you can afford such expensive shoes and handbags. They must pay well at the clinic."

"What can I say? I'm appreciated." She opened the door for him and watched him walk away without turning around in one last sentimental gesture.

Even following a late night, Lennox was still in his office before

Wednesday. She acknowledged him with a nod before settling at her desk.

Maria Jones arrived at her office door, tapping lightly.

"I've got some bad news, I'm afraid, Boss. Damien Philpot's body was recovered from the train tracks at two this morning. It took them a while to identify the remains, but they found his provisional driving license in his jeans pocket. Doctor Carter's with the body now."

Wednesday felt like a boulder had landed on her chest, impeding her ability to breath. Lennox arrived at her door.

"I've just heard; what prompted that decision?"

"My guess is he felt cornered by the evidence. My guess is he was innocent but worried he'd take the fall for the crime."

"The killer must be rubbing their hands at the news."

"Hugo Frost let him in. Perhaps he has something more to do with this case than we initially thought."

"I'll have Arlow and Damlish bring him in."

"We don't believe you're telling us everything," Wednesday said, slamming the palm of her hand on the table.

"You've got this wrong. Damien had nothing to do with the murder, and I'm damn sure I don't either. Why would I want some old man, who I never met, dead?" His face was beaded with sweat, and the tremor in his hands was visible to all in the room.

"Why did you agree to let Damien into the hotel?"

"He is—was—a mate, and we do anything for each other."

"Even kill or protect a killer?"

"No, no, it's not like that. Damien wasn't a killer."

"So what did you think when Richie Dover was found murdered? Did you confront Damien?"

"Of course I did, but he swore he was already dead when he got there. I could tell he was frightened."

"So why didn't either of you come forward?"

"I said he'd look guilty, and Mrs P would sack me for letting him on the premises."

"Did you see him after his arrest?"

"Yeah, he came straight 'round to mine after getting out on bail. He looked really cut-up."

"Did he say anything about wanting to kill himself?"

"If he had I'd have fucking stopped him . . ." his voice cracked, and he took a laboured breath before continuing. "He was like a brother and I knew he hadn't done it, but he thought you lot did. His death is on your hands." He wiped his nose on the back of his hand.

"Did you hear, a friend of that barman killed himself after getting out on bail for that murder," Vincent said to Sandra, who was heating up a tin of soup.

"Well that'll save the tax payer money for a trial."

"But why would he do it?"

"Isobel told me his gold watch was missing. People have killed for less." She poured her soup into a two-handled mug and made her way to the lounge.

Vincent could not resist following her.

"Can't we just talk anymore? You keep running away to another room."

"Now the divorce is through, I just want you to move out. It seems you're stalling."

"My new place isn't ready, for God's sake." He stomped out of the room, muttering how he wished it was she who had been murdered.

"I heard that," she called out.

"If you believe Damien Philpot was innocent, where does that leave us?" queried Lennox.

"Back to the members of the group. My gut feeling is it's an inside job," Wednesday replied, opening up the mind map she had sketched.

Lennox tried to read it upside down, but her scrawl made it difficult to decipher.

"The only thing our two victims have in common is the divorce group; they'd never met before, or even spent time in that hotel previously."

"So if we rule out Frost and Philpot, I'd also say we also rule out Eileen Potter."

"Why, because she's older? It takes no strength at all to poison someone."

"But the stabbing would be challenging."

"So are we looking at two killers?"

Lennox shrugged. "The only motive for both murders is the peripheries around divorce; who gets what. We know Jack and Michelle Turner were fighting over who got the house and dog, and Richie and Isobel Dover were fighting over the custody of their child."

"So we're back to the spouses as they both had a considerable amount to lose, and have both gained from the deaths."

"There's something there, but I can't quite see what."

"I'll get Arlow and Damlish to dig further into the spouses' backgrounds, see what turns up."

Darkness swallowed the day outside Wednesday's office window as she sifted through the background information on the Turners and the Dovers.

Jack Turner came into money when a childless aunt left him everything. He used the money to set up a high-end estate agency. He married Michelle, and they never had children, preferring instead to own a dog and live a decadent lifestyle. She continued reading, then paused to phone Lennox.

On entering her office, he sat down, waiting to hear what was so urgent.

"Damlish dug up a criminal record for Jack Turner. He was arrested and charged at the age of twenty-two for assaulting his girlfriend. He got a suspended sentence, but then began stalking her, so he was arrested again and sent to prison for a few months. He's not the innocent man he proclaims to be."

"Okay, *he* may be capable of stabbing a man, but why the poisoning?"

"Maybe he used a different method to throw us off his trail."

"Perhaps, but listen to this. Isobel's prior boyfriend to Richie died falling from a balcony whilst at a party. It was an open verdict, as no scenario could be proven. Isobel was caught with cannabis and amphetamines in her handbag. Again, not such an innocent character."

"So Jack's demonstrated his penchant for violence, and are you suggesting Isobel may have pushed her boyfriend off the balcony?"

"I can't say that, but these revelations make me see the pair in another light, and I'd like to talk with them about it, see how they react."

"Have you news?" Jack Turner asked, letting the detectives in.

"We'd like to talk with you about something we've discovered," Wednesday replied.

Jack looked puzzled.

"We've discovered your past criminal record for assaulting and stalking a girlfriend."

"Good lord, that was thirty-five years ago. What the hell does that have to do with Michelle's death?"

"Perhaps nothing, perhaps everything. It shows you have the ability to show aggression towards women, so why not to men as well?"

"Because I've changed over the years. She was a manipulative woman, who goaded me into violence whilst I was immature and volatile."

Wednesday frowned. "Why did you stalk her?"

"Because after everything she'd put me through I thought I was in love with her, and would never find a love like that again. Seems ridiculous now, the folly of youth, I suppose."

"Were you ever violent to subsequent girlfriends, or Michelle?"

He glared at her for a few seconds, before inhaling deeply. "I learnt my lesson back then. I've never raised a hand to a woman since."

"And to a man?"

"Not that I recall."

"When is Michelle's funeral?"

"I don't know; her parents are organizing it, and naturally they don't want me present."

"Remember, Mr Turner, we do find things out eventually, so if you're hiding anything else, I suggest you speak up now."

"You've uncovered the only skeleton in my closet."

"Let's hope so, for your sake."

They left him and walked to the car through a curtain of drizzle. Wednesday tucked loose strands of hair behind her ears before climbing into the passenger seat.

"We need to find out when the funeral is; might be worth our while speaking to her family."

Isobel Dover was more accommodating than Jack, in that she offered them coffee on their arrival.

"We have a few questions about your past," Wednesday said, taking a mug of coffee from Isobel.

"Don't tell me, it's to do with Shane's death."

"According to the file his parents were convinced it wasn't an accident or suicide; they blamed you."

"He was their only child, and he could do no wrong in their eyes."

Holly toddled into the room and demanded attention from her mother, who lifted her onto her lap.

"He was found with a large amount of amphetamines in his system, and you were found with some in your handbag. His parents swore he wasn't on drugs, and blamed you for that too, saying you drugged him. They proclaimed you were a bad influence."

"What parent actually recognises their kid's on drugs? I'll know with Holly because I've been there. I didn't force him; it was *he* who got me into drugs in the first place."

"Did you say this to them?"

"Yes, and they called me a liar. They wouldn't let me go to his funeral." She hugged Holly tightly until the child tried to wriggle free.

"It wasn't long after his death that you met Richie."

"I wasn't coping with Shane's death, so I went clubbing every weekend, which is where I met him."

"Was he aware of the Shane situation?"

"It rather thrilled him. He said he liked dating a potentially dangerous woman."

"It wasn't long after you met that you fell pregnant."

"He wasn't thrilled at first; said I'd done it on purpose. And perhaps I had, I needed to feel loved."

"You got married all the same."

"His parents insisted; they wanted complete access to their first grandchild."

"And how is that with them now?"

"They're distraught and mistrusting of me. They had the nerve to say that two men died whilst with me, and I'm only twenty-six . . . Oh I see. You think I had something to do with both deaths too."

"We're not finding any outside links to his death, so we're focusing on the people in the hotel."

"I thought that lad had done it? Anyway, I suppose I had a lot to lose in the divorce which is why you're looking at me so closely. But tell me, how did I get the knife so far away when I never left the hotel?" Holly's wriggling had become intolerable, so she put her down on the carpet.

"We haven't got everything worked through as yet but we will."

"Well come back to me when you have." She stood up, stepping over her daughter and heading for the door.

"When's Richie's funeral?"

"Day after tomorrow, you can come if you want, although you might be part of a very large crowd, he was a *popular* man. It's been announced in the local paper and on the radio station he worked for, so I'm expecting a swarm of silly little girls to be there."

Wednesday and Lennox got up, placing their mugs on the table, and followed her to the front door.

"Thank you for your time," said Wednesday, stepping outside.

By the time they got back to the office, Damlish had discovered Michelle Turner's funeral was the following day; family connections had brought her a quicker funeral than Richie Dover.

Chapter 19

Befitting a funeral, the morning was cloaked in fog. Wednesday was filled with the same dread she always had before attending such an event; immortality cast a darker, deeper shadow over her as the years advanced.

Lennox arrived at her front door in time to prevent her overwhelming anxiety from paralysing her.

"You can drive," she said, swinging her front door shut behind her.

By the time they arrived at the church, the fog had dissipated, but the air still hung heavy with lingering droplets. The church was ostentatious like the appearance of Michelle Turner's family who were huddled together, their glossy black feather fascinators reminiscent of a murder of crows.

Wednesday and Lennox moved silently from the car and drifted towards the church as the coffin was being removed from the hearse. They followed the group in, deducing the parents to be the older couple at the front, gripped together in furious grief.

The congregation was compiled of a mainly older section of society, with only the odd smattering of people a similar age to Michelle. True to his word, Jack was not there. No one from the group was there either, but that may have been by design of the parents.

The granite stone church was cold and damp, leaving an eerie arm of death draping over Wednesday's shoulders. On shuddering, Lennox leant in to check she was okay.

"I just want this to be over," she whispered.

A man in front of them turned around and frowned.

The ceremony was a starchy affair, but mercifully short in length. As Michelle was to be interned, Wednesday and Lennox hung back until the graveside vigil was over, and people began drifting away towards their cars.

As the detectives wandered over, the parents' faces clouded over, until realising they were members of the police force they were expecting to see.

"Do come back to our home, there is much we want to talk about," said Mr Reynolds.

The Reynolds' house was bedecked with large bouquets of fresh, fragrant peace lilies in every room.

"Michelle loved fresh flowers," said Mrs Reynolds, noticing Wednesday's regard. "I bet *he* didn't buy them for her." A fat tear swelled before dropping down her line-ravaged cheek.

Mr Reynolds put his arm around his wife's shoulders and directed her to a concerned-looking woman sitting on the sofa, before turning around and beckoning them into his study. Closing the door behind them, he sighed deeply before sitting on a high-backed chair behind a small leather-topped desk.

"This has hit us very hard, detectives. Outliving one's child should never happen to a parent. Do you have children?" he asked, looking directly at Wednesday.

"I don't, but we're very sorry for your loss. You said you had lots to say to us."

"I didn't want to talk in front of the guests; they don't know how it's been."

The detectives sat down opposite him and waited.

"Jack had lots of money when he was dating Michelle, but shortly after they married, he lost most of his fortune on the stock exchange. Instead of allowing us to help them, he alienated Michelle from us, and made her go to work whist he tried to make a go of his estate agency with the last of his money. He was so controlling."

"Couldn't she leave him?" Lennox asked.

"She said she loved him. What do women know about love?" He shook his head slowly. "Anyway, his agency soon became successful, but Michelle chose to keep working. Doris was convinced it was Michelle's only way to get some freedom, financially and socially."

"Do you remember where she worked?"

"We went there, after a friend said he'd seen her in an auction house, where it transpired she was the office manager. She was so cold towards us, saying that all we wanted to do was come between her and Jack. He'd brainwashed her."

"Was that the last time you spoke with her?" Wednesday asked, keen to move things along.

"No, she contacted us about three months ago to say she was seeking a divorce. She said she was no longer in love with him, and that she'd met someone else at work."

"Did she give you a name?"

"No, but she did say Jack didn't want a divorce, and if she planned to go ahead with it, he wouldn't just hand over the house and Jasper."

"Did he know she'd met someone else?"

"I don't know for sure; I don't think so."

He looked drained, and Wednesday thought he should get back to his wife.

"That was very helpful, thank you. We'll get back to you if we have further questions."

On opening the door, the muted buzz of the milling family came as a stark contrast to the stillness of the past few ragged minutes. Mrs Reynolds was nowhere in sight, so they slipped out without causing a ripple to the atmosphere.

"That's a different story to Jack's version of events," commented Lennox as he unlocked the car. "He made out it was a mutual parting; do you think he knew about Michelle's new beau?"

Wednesday let out a pig-like snort. "Who uses the word *beau* these days?"

"I think the Reynolds' have rubbed off on me, with their nineteen-fifties decor and mannerisms."

"We need to find out if Jack knew or not, but he's not going to tell us. Let's ask Carl or Stella if he did. Then we'll try and find the man at the auction house to see whether Michelle confided in him how Jack was really treating her."

Carl and Stella were meeting at her place to discuss the forthcoming new Parting Ways group. Carl had tried putting the detectives off joining them, but Wednesday was insistent.

Stella opened her front door and directed them to the lounge where they found Carl pouring over the application forms spread over the table. He presented them with a forced smile, knowing they would recognise it as such.

"Had Michelle mentioned she was in love with someone else?" asked Wednesday, scanning their faces for their initial twitches.

Both facilitators looked surprised.

"According to her father, she'd informed them three months prior to that weekend, but he wasn't sure if Jack knew."

"Michelle was quite a flirtatious woman; you must have noticed her interest in you, DS Lennox," Carl said, "so it's not that surprising. However, whether Jack knew, I'm afraid I can't say."

"I always sensed there was more to their story," piped up Stella, "but neither of them was forthcoming with the truth; whatever that may be." She shuffled the forms into a pile. "Jack did seem deeply angry about something, but he wasn't one to share in group sessions. What about the one-to-one time with you?" she continued, turning to Carl.

"I know he was angry with Michelle's solicitor for saying she had to remain in the house so as not to lose any rights over it."

"Is that true?" Lennox queried.

Carl shrugged. "As Stella said, he wasn't one for sharing. When the other men did, he scorned their openness and said some things were better left private."

"Did Michelle say much?" Wednesday asked Stella, who was gazing out the window.

"She did mention that a loveless marriage was the loneliest place to be. She said she'd rather be single than living with Jack."

"Did she ever mention him being violent?"

"I always bring this topic to the foreground in sessions; I think I need to offer an opening on such a difficult subject. Having said that, Michelle only mentioned she was afraid of his verbal temper."

Wednesday felt they were only scratching the surface of the Turners' relationship, and needed time to assimilate the new ground.

"I don't suppose anything within these boundaries was mentioned regarding the Dovers, was it?"

"Another loveless marriage, I'm afraid," Carl replied. "Although I'm sure it won't be long until Isobel's found a new man."

"What makes you say that?"

"She's young and attractive."

"Did she mention if anyone else was on the scene?"

"She was extremely against people having affairs; compounded I imagine by her husband's philandering. She saw it as a highest sin against the sanctity of marriage."

"Enough for her to do or wish him harm?"

"Not in the manner you're implying, Inspector."

Wednesday felt they had squeezed the last drops of information from the facilitators, and bid them goodbye. Tomorrow was yet another funeral, and she needed some time with her parents to remind her that there is life before death, even if her mother's life was somewhat chaotic. It was all she had.

Oliver greeted her with a bear hug, as Wednesday stood on the doorstep.

"You look tired," he said. "Are you looking after yourself?"

"As much as possible. How's Mum?"

"Doing well; come see for yourself."

They wandered into the brightly lit kitchen to find Joan at her easel, engrossed in painting. The sight lifted Wednesday's spirit, until Joan saw her and asked if she had brought her boyfriend with her.

"Mum, Lennox is—"

Joan burst into a ripple of laughter. "I'm only teasing you, even though I wish he were."

"Two reasons it'll never happen: one, we work together, and two, he dated Scarlett."

"You shouldn't write him off for either of those reasons; he's a good man, and I'm sure he cares for you."

Wednesday pulled the same face she used as a stroppy teenager, so Joan knew it was time to move on.

"Did Oliver tell you he's been accepted by the Cambridge craft fair? He'll have his own stall. Won't that be fun?"

"You should try for one of your own next time."

"If only I was guaranteed to be sane enough around the time," she smiled weakly. "I think I'll just revel in his success."

The evening progressed smoothly, but the case bubbled away at the back of Wednesday's mind, affecting her appetite, which did not go unnoticed. Oliver interspersed the evening by regaling them with village gossip until it was time for her to leave.

She arrived home, listening to her apprehensive thoughts about attending yet another funeral in the morning.

Chapter 20

Wednesday was still upstairs when Lennox arrived to collect her. She patted the subtle bulge under her chin, before cantering downstairs.

He knew better than to ask how she was, as they sat in his car, heading for the crematorium.

On their arrival, they spotted the local news team hovering on the pavement, gearing up to garner news and quotes about the local celebrity. Small clusters of young women, dressed as though going clubbing, hugged each other in front of the camera crew, hoping to grab a few minutes of fame. Each woman held a single red rose, ready to throw at the funeral cortege.

"Isobel's going to be delighted," Lennox commented, his eyes lingering a tad too long on the women.

"I'm sure she's expecting it; she said as much."

The camera crew turned to face them as they got out of the car. A man brandishing a microphone galloped towards them, cameraman in tow.

"Are there any developments in the case? Do you think the killer will be here today?" he asked, breathily.

"No comment," Wednesday said tersely, before forging onwards with Lennox by her side.

In the distance, they saw a few familiar faces gathered by the entrance. Carl was the first one to see them, raising his hand in a discreet greeting. Tamara was standing by his side. As they got closer, the rest of the group came into view.

"We've come to support Isobel," said Stella as they reached her. "I hope she's not too upset by the media attention; she's quite a private person."

"Hopefully she'll ignore them as we did," replied Wednesday.

Stella's gaze travelled over Wednesday's shoulder, and on turning, Wednesday saw the black cars creeping into the crematorium grounds with red roses bouncing off the car bonnet as the women offered their final gesture of admiration to Richie.

"We ought to go in," Paul said, edging his way inside.

The detectives followed the group inside, and positioned themselves at the back; noting who was not there. Hugo Frost, Tim Binder, and Megan Hart were all absent, but the rest of the group was complete, including Jack Turner.

When the coffin entered the building, the song "Perfect Day," by Lou Reed, played. Wednesday did not know whether he genuinely liked the song or whether it was a blunt message from Isobel. Either way it seemed an odd choice.

Isobel followed the coffin, wearing a poppy-red dress and carrying Holly in her arms. The child looked restless, and Wednesday wondered how long it would be before she was running up and down the aisle. Isobel's pinched face looked straight ahead.

The detectives looked around to see who else would arrive, but Isobel had demanded a private service for family and close friends, so the press and grieving fans were shut outside.

Tamara was the only member of the group who looked around. Catching Wednesday's gaze, she offered a wilted smile. Everyone else held their head low until the service was over. Once again, "Perfect Day" played as the coffin rolled smoothly along the track before thick, red-velvet curtains swished closed, shielding onlookers from the final destination.

Isobel stood up as Holly tugged on the hem of her dress.

"You're all welcome back to my house for a drink and nibbles." Her smile faded as she caught sight of Wednesday.

Outside, the sun had come out, kissing the heads of all the red-eyed mourners. Holly made a quick getaway, but Stella managed to catch the girl's trailing arm as she scurried past. The girl looked up, scowling at her captor.

Caterers were already waiting for everyone as they arrived. Flutes of sparkling wine on silver trays were offered to each person as they entered. The detectives waved the trays away.

"I imagine you're surprised to see me here," said Jack Turner as he levelled with them. "I couldn't attend yesterday, but I thought there was no reason why I shouldn't attend today. He wasn't a bad fellow, as it happens."

"We did attend yesterday, and we'd like to talk to you about it. Today isn't appropriate. Could you come to the station tomorrow?"

Jack's face flushed as he agreed to their request before taking a glass of wine, downing it rapidly, and moving on.

Isobel was talking animatedly to Stella, who was still holding Holly's hand. In between talking, she was drinking her wine rapidly, and replacing her glass just as fast.

"How are you coping with the day?" Wednesday asked as they approached the pair.

"It's lovely to see everyone from the hotel again, but I assume you're asking more how it feels to have said a final goodbye to Richie," Isobel replied, grabbing another glass from a passing tray. "I'd be lying if I said I was upset; we were divorcing, after all. But I'm sorry Holly's lost her father."

"Interesting choice of music in the crematorium."

"Richie saw himself as a bit of a Lou Reed persona; he played the part a fair bit on his show. Nothing as awful as you probably thought, eh?"

"I'm not here to judge you."

"Well I don't rightly care what people think. They only had to look at those pathetic young girls throwing flowers at his cold, dead body to see he wasn't the devoted family-man he made out he was."

Stella put her hand on Isobel's arm. "Everyone here is supporting *you*."

"That's right," said Sandra Vine, appearing next to them holding a small plate piled with vol-au-vents and mini quiches. "I hear Michelle was buried yesterday, but I wouldn't have attended hers."

"Why not?" queried Wednesday.

"Because she was an embarrassment to the female species. I mean, the way she flirted with you," she said, looking at Lennox, "made her look ridiculous. She was old enough to know better."

"She appeared harmless and was soon to be a single woman anyway," retorted Wednesday, feeling the hairs on the back of her neck rise.

"She thought she was above us; quite snooty at times."

"My ex showing her softer side," joked Vincent, arriving to join the group.

Wednesday ignored his comment and moved away with Lennox at her elbow. She spied Eileen Potter standing by the table of food, piling the treats on her plate.

"I'm surprised to see you here," said Wednesday.

"I may not have approved of their actions, but that doesn't mean I wished any of them dead. Besides, I thought I'd look rude if I didn't accept the invitation." She popped a mini quiche into her mouth before turning away.

Lennox was about to speak, but was prevented by Wednesday nudging him.

"Let's get back," she said, taking one last look at Isobel, who was enjoying being the centre of attention to Carl, Paul, and Jack, noticing the latter had his arm around Isobel's waist. He withdrew it swiftly as he caught her eye.

Jack arrived at the station and was led into the interview room to await Wednesday and Lennox.

"We need to tread carefully with this man," Wednesday stated before finishing her mug of tepid coffee. "I think he's been quite clever in not revealing too much about his feelings."

"That's also a man thing," Lennox replied.

"Not all men bury their wives one day, and fawn all over another woman the very next day."

"They were divorcing, Boss. Besides, he may just have been comforting her."

At that moment, Maria Jones arrived and informed Wednesday that Stella Hibit was on the phone, saying it was urgent.

"DI Wednesday."

"I'm sorry to bother you, but something troubled me yesterday, and I didn't see what it was until today. Jack always had a soft spot for Isobel. I thought it was a fatherly role, but yesterday after the funeral, he seemed . . . well . . . rather overly attentive towards her."

"And you're troubled by this because?"

"What happens if she rebuffs him? Is he a danger to women in that circumstance? Did he kill Michelle because she wanted to leave him and he doesn't take rejection well?"

"Thank you for contacting us; I will bear your concerns in mind." She put the receiver down before Stella could press her further.

She relayed the conversation to Lennox on the way to the interview room.

Jack was nursing a plastic cup of weak tea when they entered. Wednesday sat directly opposite him with Lennox by her side. The smell of a previous nervous occupant lingered in the air.

"As you know, we met Michelle's family after her funeral, and they were quite negative about you," Wednesday said flatly.

"That's not surprising; I was divorcing their little darling."

"They were under the impression that it was Michelle who'd instigated the divorce."

"What do they know about anything; Michelle hadn't spoken to them for years."

"Actually, she'd contacted them about three months ago, and told them her plans."

"They're lying," he spat. "She would have told me if she had."

"They also said you were very controlling in the relationship; that when you lost most of your inheritance, you refused their help and sent Michelle out to work instead."

"I see you believe their fabrications. They're bitter because she chose me over them."

"They also mentioned Michelle had found someone else; someone from work whom she was in love with."

Jack's head tipped backwards as he let out a theatrical laugh. "She was incapable of love. I think she only married me to crawl out of their clutches. They were overbearing; always out to cause trouble between us. They're still trying to cause trouble now."

"Did you know she'd met someone else?"

Turner paused. "I suspected, but I didn't know for sure. He was welcome to her in any case. She wasn't an easy woman to live with, she expected too much out of life."

"Did you choose not to have children?"

"She was too selfish for that. She wanted to be the centre of attention, and a mother always has to put her offspring first."

"Did *you* want children?"

"No, it suited me not to at the time."

"What are you going to do with your life now?"

"My business has ridden the recession, and I'm now a widower with everything to look forward to. I'm not going to lie to you; I didn't kill her, but I'd stopped loving her, so I can't pretend to be grieving." He sat back and looked at them both before draining the plastic cup of tea.

"Have you any plans on seeing Isobel now both funerals are over?"

"Isobel? Why do you think I'd be interested in her?"

"Comments from other members of the group, and from our own observations yesterday. You seemed very close to her, perhaps you've both already discussed this issue?"

"I don't see what this has to do with anything, but seeing as it seems to interest you, yes, Isobel is beautiful and charming, and of course I'd like to take her out to dinner to see how we'd get along away from the glare of the group, but no, we don't have any plans currently. Satisfied?"

Wednesday nodded before an officer escorted him out.

"We should visit the auction house tomorrow to see if we can trace Michelle's love-interest," Wednesday said before they headed for their respective offices.

Lennox watched her from behind his desk, wondering who she was talking to on her mobile phone. Smiling at his own curiosity, he decided he needed to get out more.

Chapter 21

Scarlett entered the kitchen looking seductively bedraggled thanks to the droplets of drizzle cloaking her hair and coat. She threw her coat over a chair, tossing droplets around like miniscule shards of diamonds.

Wednesday watched her half-sister smoking by the back door, admiring her flame hair glistening as it billowed over her shoulders, forming a ghostly mantel.

"Harriet's left me," she said, smoke seeping from between her lips.

"I didn't know you had a new girlfriend."

"I didn't say anything as I didn't want to jinx it, but she left me anyway."

"How are you feeling?"

Scarlett took another deep drag. "Wretched and guilty. People always leave me, and they all say the same thing." She studied the burning tip of the cigarette.

Wednesday waited, pouring two small glasses of wine, one topped up with lemonade, before placing it near Scarlett.

"They all say I'm too difficult to be with. My mood swings and sometimes pathological jealousy pushes them away." Stubbing out her cigarette on the ground, she threw it into the garden before picking up her wine glass. "Do you still worry about your sanity?"

Wednesday nodded. "I'm finding it hard to hold it together at times. Sometimes I'm overwhelmed by the thought of madness seeping into my mind. Is your mental health bothering you currently?"

Scarlett closed the back door and moved to the table, her shadow rippling on the wall from the candles on the table.

"I'm constantly terrified, actually. Since diagnosis, I see nothing but madness in every action I make."

"Are you taking your meds correctly?"

"Of course, I see what it does to Mum."

"Then give yourself time to settle."

"Settling is not something I anticipate doing any time soon."

"You have Oliver and me to turn to when things get tough."

"I'm not sure Dad or you can cope with two mad women in your lives."

Wednesday sighed, picking at the cheese sandwich she had made earlier. "We'll manage; we love you both."

"Maybe," shrugged Scarlett, pushing her barely-touched glass away. "I don't think alcohol helps me, even though I know you dilute it, but I'm just so tired. I'm not sleeping well."

"Go and have a relaxing bath. The evening's never a good time to dwell on things."

She left a shadow of gloom as she disappeared upstairs. Wednesday's shoulders hunched over as she threw her sandwich in the bin before picking up her laptop.

Curling up on the sofa, she typed "bipolar affective disorder" in the search engine, and began reading. Scholarly articles were sometimes too difficult to comprehend, but she dismissed any article purporting to cure the disorder with herbal remedies.

The more she read, the more she saw Scarlett's behavioural pattern displayed on the screen. Two things struck her: pervasive sleep disturbance was a characteristic of the disorder with difficulties in regulating mood being another. She had much to learn about this particular disorder if she was going to offer Scarlett the support she required.

Scarlett was moving around upstairs, her bath seemingly over. Wednesday sighed, closing her laptop before trooping upstairs.

"Would you like to move back in with me for a while?" she asked, watching Scarlett deftly wrapping her hair up in a towel.

"Taking pity on me?"

"I'm worried about you. I don't like seeing you like this."

A mottled red rash clambered up Scarlett's neck.

"Also, I'm lonely at times, and find the house too quiet. We had some good times."

Scarlett smiled wanly. "I suppose it wouldn't hurt for a while. Just until I get on top of whatever's bothering me."

Wednesday left Scarlett to go to bed and returned downstairs, knowing that sleep would be alluding her for a while.

The auction house was situated nine miles north of Cambridge. It was a large barn conversion set amongst arable farmland, with ample parking to the front. Lennox pulled on the handbrake and then turned to Wednesday.

"You've been quiet all morning, and I think I know you well enough by now to know something's wrong."

"You're very perceptive," she smiled. "If you must know, I've invited Scarlett to move back in with me for a while; I'm worried about her."

"A blast from my past. Sorry. Is it serious or just Scarlett being Scarlett?"

"Both, I suppose. Anyway, let's get on with this."

They walked directly into the large salesroom. Antique furniture, oil paintings, and canteens of silver cutlery filled the wood-scented space. Eager people wandered around, scribbling down notes on the auction house brochure and whispering behind cupped hands.

As they wandered up to the reception desk, a woman held out two brochures.

"I'm DI Wednesday and this is DS Lennox. Are you the owner?"

"One of the owners, Emma Wiseman; my brother and sister are the other partners. Has something happened?"

"We're making enquiries regarding Michelle Turner."

The woman put her hand over her heart. "Poor Michelle, it was such a shock. Do you know how it happened?"

"How did Michelle get on with everyone here?"

Emma smiled. "I see you're not here for chit-chat, and I know what you're getting at. You want to know if she was especially close to anyone."

"And was she?"

"Perhaps you'd like to meet him?" She made a call on the phone.

"Donald Wiseman," he said, walking up to them with an outstretched hand. "I understand you're here about Michelle."

"Is there somewhere we can talk privately?"

He took them through reception and into a poky office at the back that smelt of tarnished silver and moth balls.

"Were you in a relationship with Michelle?"

"I thought she was beautiful when she came for the interview, but I knew she was married. However, it didn't take long to find out she was unhappy. We went out for a few drinks; the rest you can work out for yourselves."

"Did she tell her husband?"

"I'm not sure. I think she was afraid of how he'd react."

"Had he been violent towards her?"

"Not physically, but verbally. He terrified her at times. I offered to go with her, but she refused."

"Had she nowhere else to go?"

"She wouldn't leave her house or dog, and we weren't that serious. Perhaps we would have been, given time, but . . ."

"Did her husband ever visit here?"

"Not that I know of, but we get a lot of people milling around. Do you suspect he's the one who killed her?"

"We're just building a profile of the victim. Thank you for your time." Wednesday rose from her seat, and Lennox followed suit.

"It would have made it easier if he knew she'd told Jack. As it is, we've got nowhere to go, and nothing to hang on him."

Climbing back into the car, Lennox toyed with a packet of cigarettes in his coat pocket. He missed the days of smoking together and had noticed her wrinkling her nose after he had smoked. Maybe it was his turn to quit. Then he remembered his sons.

"Will I still be welcome in your home after Scarlett's moved back?"

"Of course, as long as you refrain from seducing her again. Not for my sake, you understand, but for hers."

"Don't worry, that won't be happening."

They arrived back at the station to find Alex hovering outside her office.

"Just the people, I have some news," he smiled, brandishing a sheet of paper. "I contacted a specialist botanist regarding Michelle Turner's poisoning. I sent her a sample of Turner's stomach contents, and she was able to narrow down the regions where the belladonna was sourced."

"Excellent," exclaimed Wednesday, grateful of the distraction.

They entered her office.

"She studied the soil composition via the plant, and suggests you look in Essex and Hertfordshire, around waste spaces, quarries, or near old ruins."

Wednesday's face fell. "That's not narrow enough. They're vast counties."

"That's why you're the inspector and I'm not." He smiled and departed.

"Do you miss the attention he used to give you?" asked Lennox.

"We've got more important things to worry about."

"That's a *yes* then."

She threw a pencil at him as he retreated hastily to his office.

Carl handed Megan a brown envelope. She peered into it.

"This doesn't look like enough," she said, screwing-up her face.

"It's all I can manage at a time. People will notice it missing if I take too much at once."

"It's not coming fast enough. I can't leave the country on what you've given me so far."

Carl sighed. "You're never going to stop blackmailing me, are you?"

"You're such a cynic for a counsellor; a man of little faith. When I have enough between you and the house sale, I'll be out of your hair."

"I'm not sure I can believe that. Besides, I'm not sure my behaviour warrants all this hassle."

"You must have believed it at one point, otherwise you'd have told me to back off at the start. It's the potential damage it could do to your career that drives you."

"You're a hard woman, for a nurse."

"Nurses aren't *actual* angels. I have my dark side like anyone else."

He rose from the bench and headed to the park exit, his hands shoved in his pockets and his head hung low. His demeanour meant he did not see Tamara standing behind the black railings, watching the scene very closely.

As Megan began opening her front door, she received a sharp shove in her back, propelling her inside and sending her crashing to the floor.

Chapter 22

Tamara closed the front door behind her before placing her foot between Megan's shoulder blades, putting her weight on Megan's petite frame, and squeezing the air out of her victim's lungs.

"Who are you?" gasped Megan. "What do you want?"

"I want *you* to keep away from my man," Tamara hissed through gritted teeth.

Bending down, she grasped a handful of Megan's hair, yanking her head back. Megan squealed, reaching for Tamara's hand.

"You don't understand," she gasped. "It's not what you think. Please . . ." she pleaded, as Tamara's full weight crushed her into the laminate floor.

"Save it, bitch; I've heard it all before from other women. You're not the first to think they can wheedle their way into his life. I'm enough woman for him."

Megan was desperate. "Is that why he likes young men?"

Tamara's grip tightened. "What are you talking about?"

Megan tried to hold her hair at the roots to ease her pain, but Tamara batted her away with her free hand.

"I work at a private clinic. It's not all cosmetic surgery; it deals with sexual health too. I did a few shifts there."

Tamara rolled her over, straddling her so they were face to face. "Go on."

"Carl came in a while back, before the group met. He'd contracted Chlamydia and was advised to tell everyone he'd slept with. He panicked, and that's when I discovered his penchant for young men."

Tamara released her hair, and straightened up. She remained in place, but her eyes betrayed her inner turmoil.

"Are you telling me he's bisexual? Or are you creating a cover story for your affair and trying to get me to leave him?" she hissed, spraying Megan's face with spittle.

"I swear it's true. I wanted to get enough money out of him to get away from here, that's all."

Lifting herself off Megan's torso, Tamara moved away and leant against the wall. She watched Megan slowly lift up onto her elbows; each woman's eyes unflinchingly fixed on the other.

"He never told me," she said finally.

"You should get yourself checked out."

"How long ago was this?"

"About seven months."

"I've been trying to get pregnant for the past five months," she said flatly, holding her hand against her stomach. "Chlamydia can make you infertile if untreated, can't it?"

Megan nodded, slowly rising to her feet. "Does he know you're trying?"

Tamara shook her head, sinking to the floor, now placing herself in a vulnerable position. Megan contemplated her moves, but assessed her assailant was emotionally coshed.

"I could get you an appointment if you want. Privately, of course."

"As privately as Carl's," she replied snidely.

Megan held out her hands, palms up. "Desperate times call for desperate measures."

She walked over to Tamara, offering her a hand to stand. Finally, they were both face to face, and Megan was no longer afraid. Perhaps she had finally found an ally.

Wednesday had asked Arlow and Damlish to sift through the suspects' lives to see any connection to Essex or Hertfordshire. It was a long shot, but Hunter was pressing her for results.

"He's bad tempered these days; that's what divorce does to you," Lennox said, spooning coffee granules into two mugs.

"You should know, but it doesn't make working with him any easier. I've got compassion fatigue," replied Wednesday.

"Take him out for a drink. It would do you both good."

"I'll pretend I didn't hear that." Snatching her mug from the table, she hastened to her office and shut the door.

As she bit into a chocolate bar, her mobile rang. It was Oliver.

"Have you seen Scarlett?" he asked.

"She's staying with me. I've asked her to move back in."

"Thank heavens," he sighed, his breath sounding like that of a vexed bull. "I'm worried about her."

"More than usual?"

"Work called here, wondering if we knew where she was. She hasn't been at work for the past two weeks. The editor's not happy."

"I'll sort it out, don't worry. How's Mum?"

"Anxious about Scarlett, which isn't helping matters."

Wednesday rubbed her forehead. "Tell her not to worry, and tell her Scarlett's safe at home with me." Dropping her mobile into her handbag, she turned her attention to the computer screen, hoping to find some inspiration, but she was distracted by Damlish standing at her door. She beckoned him in.

"I've collated some details from all the interviews, Boss. Thought you'd like them ASAP."

She nodded in the direction of the chair for him to take a seat.

"Carl Trott and Tamara Jackson like skiing holidays, playing squash, and long hikes, to de-clutter their minds, apparently." He looked at her, rolling his eyes. "We need to find out where exactly they hike."

Wednesday made a note. Damlish waited before going on.

"Stella Hibit loves finding old churches to photograph."

"That's where I saw all those black and white photos; very atmospheric." She made another note.

"Jack Turner likes fly-fishing, and he sells mansions with things like follies in large grounds, and Vincent Vine still goes on scouting holidays to places in the wilderness. They're the main people to focus on."

"Good work," she said, dismissing him and picking up her phone. "Let's visit Carl and Tamara," she said, simultaneously picking up her bag and slamming her desk drawer shut with her knee.

They followed Carl into his lounge and took a seat on the sofa as he walked to the window overlooking the garden, his hands clasped behind his back.

"She's not here," he said.

"When's she returning?" asked Wednesday, irritated by the view of his back.

"I don't know. She wasn't here when I got in."

"You seem troubled by that," commented Wednesday. "Does this often happen."

"I don't know what you're implying," he replied, turning round, "but Tamara and I are a happy, united couple, who don't have secrets."

"I often find the people who say that, are often the ones in trouble," Lennox said with a wry smile.

Carl turned back to face the garden, rising up and down on the balls of his feet. "Says the divorced man who dresses to impress."

Lennox was about to retort, when Wednesday placed her hand on his arm.

"Where exactly did you go on your last holiday?"

"We went to the Alps, skiing for ten days. Why?"

"No long hikes recently?"

"Unfortunately not; we've both been too busy . . ."

The sound of the front door opening and closing interrupted him.

He stepped forward as Tamara mounted the stairs before entering the lounge.

"I see we have visitors," she said, blushing. "Has he offered you a drink?"

"We're fine," replied Wednesday. "He was just telling us about your last holiday."

"Did he tell you how he got so pissed on glühwein, he had to be carried to bed by two burly men?" she laughed. "But perhaps he didn't tell you because he secretly enjoyed it?" She smiled at him with one eyebrow raised, which he took as a foreboding sign.

"I'm sure the detectives don't need to know about that."

"What, more secrets for you to keep?" she purred.

Carl's face paled beneath his false tan.

"Are these secrets to do with the murders," Wednesday asked, irritation fizzing up her spine.

"I don't know what she's talking about," Carl said calmly.

"Nothing to do with the crimes, but then again, who knows?" Tamara added.

"You're being very cryptic," Wednesday said, standing up. "If we find you've been hampering the investigations, you will be charged with obstruction." She walked towards Carl, and indicated for him to sit down. She waited until he had settled.

"Now, you both mentioned your love of long hikes, so please tell us the places you go."

Carl cleared his throat, but Tamara spoke first.

"We like the Fens in north Cambridgeshire, walks to Ely, and to Devil's Dyke. Nothing remarkable. Don't forget we like skiing and playing squash. Perhaps we murdered someone with our rackets."

"Tam," Carl exclaimed, "this isn't a laughing matter."

"I'm not laughing."

Wednesday indicated to Lennox they were going.

"I suggest you two sort out whatever issues you have, so when we next meet you can engage with us more honestly." She strode downstairs and out the front door without waiting for their response.

"Those two irritate the hell out of me," she said, slamming the car door.

Lennox winced, stroking the steering wheel. "I get the feeling they're not as happy as they like to make out. Relationships, eh?"

Wednesday did not bite, preferring to send a text, which he saw her do. He was tempted to ask, but her pinched mouth dissuaded him.

Rising swiftly from the chair, Carl paced to the fireplace, placing his hands on the marble mantle, his knuckles turning white.

"What the crap was that all about? It sounded like you wanted us to look guilty of something. What's got into you, Tam?"

"Wouldn't you like to know?"

"What kind of dumb question is that? Of course I want to know."

"All in good time, sweetheart, all in good time."

Wednesday and Lennox pulled up outside the Vines' house in time to see Sandra arrive armed with shopping bags. She saw them and waved gingerly with an elbow.

Chapter 23

Wednesday noted the designer bags Sandra slung on the floor and wondered where she got the finances for such high-end shops.

"Vincent was a tight-fisted sod, always moaning even if I bought a cheap top from the market. Now we're finally divorced, and my solicitor discovered the extent of his hidden wealth, I've got the money to splash out," Sandra said, noticing Wednesday eyeing the bags.

"Has he moved out?" she asked.

"He's moved in with our eldest son, his uptight wife, and two stroppy teenagers. I don't envy him," she laughed.

"Where did you go when you went on scout camping trips?"

Sandra raised her eyebrows. "Bizarre question, but I seem to remember we went to the New Forest, and Epping Forest. Bloody awful times, but it was the only way to get a holiday with our kids. I have few fond memories of our time together, but I was financially dependent on him. How times have changed," she laughed again.

"I know the first place is in Hampshire, but where's Epping Forest?"

"In Essex, Boss," Lennox interjected.

"When did you last go?"

"Vincent went earlier this year. Why the interest?"

"Ongoing investigation."

"If you want more details, you'll need to speak with him. I'll give you our Noel's address," she said, grabbing a notepad from the telephone table and scribbling down the details.

"Did Vincent talk much about Isobel Dover to you?"

Sandra handed the paper to Wednesday. "Do you mean, did he taunt me with how much younger, more beautiful, and more captivating she was? What do you think? All the men did, especially Jack. He was smitten, according to Michelle."

The detectives left and headed to the nightclub where Richie worked; Damlish had arranged an appointment with the owner.

The nightclub had grotty exterior with graffiti on the door and cigarette butts littering the pavement. Lennox pressed the intercom, announcing who they were down the crackling line.

It took a few seconds for their eyes to adjust to the dim light inside, just in time to see a thick-necked man, the height of Lennox, striding towards them.

"I'll take you to Mr Tower's office," he said gruffly.

Brendan Tower's office was lined with full-length mirrors, interspersed with screens streaming live feeds from the dance floor, chill-out lounge, and bar area. An orchid in a black pot adorned his large desk, where he sat with an unlit cigar in his mouth.

"I understand you want a chat about Richie Dover," he said without standing.

"We'd like to know whether he had any problems with anyone here, or the clientele," Wednesday asked, trying to avoid her reflection in the mirrors.

"Not with the staff, but it wouldn't surprise me if he'd pissed off some men here or there. He was a huge hit with the ladies, and he knew it. He'd have a different one up in his music zone every night."

"So some of these women weren't single?"

"Most of them, I'd guess, going by how many men were chucked out each evening after trying to start a fight with him."

"Did any of them wait for him outside?"

"You'd have to ask Scott; he mans the door."

"Was it well known he was married but unfaithful?"

"God yes, even his wife knew."

"How do you know that?"

"She came here a few months ago and caught him at his mixing-desk with two women draped over him. She went nuts. She dragged the two women away by their hair, then proceeded to have a huge row with him whilst beating him around the head with a hairbrush. Scott rescued him and chucked her out."

"You didn't involve the police?"

"He didn't want us to; said it was embarrassing enough. I barred her though."

"Did any of these girls turn into more than a one-night stand?"

Brendan searched the ceiling, his gaze falling upon a cobweb hammock straddling a corner. He frowned. "Several, although I can only remember the last one's name, Mandy something. Mandy Brook, that's it, 'cause he said she babbled on a bit too much at times."

Wednesday thanked him for his time, relieved to be leaving the mirrors behind.

"I'll contact the station to find this Mandy Brook's address. You can drive us to Jack Turner's," Wednesday said to Lennox, fastening her seatbelt.

"Going somewhere?" Wednesday asked, noticing Jack's pale pink polo top, beige chinos, and overpowering whiff of aftershave.

"I forgot you were coming, it can wait."

"Good, we need a frank discussion with you."

Stepping back, he ushered them in and through to the lounge, where Wednesday noticed all the decorative cushions had been removed from the sofa and chairs.

"We'd like an honest discussion about your feelings towards Isobel Dover. You understand this may put you in a bad light as you're a link between both murders."

Jack's face drained of all colour. Leaning forward, he hung his head low, clutching both knees with his arms.

"Are you all right?" Wednesday asked.

"No, I feel bloody awful." He looked up at her, his face shiny with sweat. "I admit, I'm a bit of a fool, and yes, I do harbour feelings for Isobel, but what would have been the point in murdering Richie? They were getting divorced."

"He had the upper hand in the settlement projections. Perhaps you felt—or she felt—she deserved more."

"I knew nothing of their settlement."

"You'd be the only one then; everybody else was aware, it was a frequent topic of conversation according to the facilitators," Wednesday sniped.

Jack threw an angry stare. "I didn't listen half the time." He sat back in his chair, sighing deeply. "I never discussed my feelings with Isobel, fearing rejection, I suppose."

"I'd like to know where your recent house sales have been. I can check the details, so you might as well tell the truth straight off."

"Property sales? Are you checking on my accounts now?"

"No, just the locations."

Jack rose and strolled over to a walnut desk positioned in an alcove. Pulling out a drawer, he removed a black leather Mulberry folder containing property details before returning to his seat.

"The recession hit the market for a while, but things are finally looking up. These past two months I've sold expensive properties in Huntington, Ely, and Hitchin. I have three more on the market in Cambridge, Ely, and Baldock. Care to look?" he asked, sliding the glossy details across the coffee table.

Picking them up, she slipped them into her bag.

"So you cover Cambridgeshire *and* Hertfordshire."

"I had to spread the net wider; Cambridgeshire itself wasn't enough, especially during these tough times."

"We'll need to see you again in due course, so don't travel far," she said, rising from the sofa.

They left and climbed into Lennox's car.

"I know I shouldn't say this, but I miss you smoking," he said, switching on the engine.

"I admit I miss our times in the courtyard, but I don't miss standing out in the cold, the smell on my clothes and hair, and the niggling voice in my head telling me I'm polluting my body. You could join me if you want."

"I will, one day."

"If you're waiting for life to run more smoothly, you'll be waiting a long time. Anyone with family will say the same. If I waited for mine to be calmer, I'd still be smoking into my nineties."

"Talking of family, how's Scarlett?"

"Being Scarlett."

"I'm sure she is," he smiled.

Mandy Brook answered the front door and let Wednesday and Lennox in, taking them to the kitchen where a rotund man sat at the table wearing a white muscle t-shirt and reading a newspaper.

"Dad, it's the police about poor Richie."

"Fuck *poor* Richie; good fucking riddance. Pardon my French."

"*Dad*, you don't want 'em thinking you had something to do with it," she muttered through gritted teeth.

"I sense strong animosity, Mr Brook," said Wednesday, sitting down next to him.

"It's Ron, and what?"

"You didn't like him."

"Damn right. Gets my Mandy pregnant and dumps her."

Mandy screwed up her eyes; her hands clenched in fists by her sides.

Wednesday turned her attention to her.

"You were pregnant? What happened?"

"We had unprotected sex," the girl replied, rolling her eyes.

"I *meant* what happened when he found out?"

"He went crazy, told me I was a stupid little girl and that I had to get rid—"

"And did you?"

"He paid for it, so I had to." She cast her gaze to the floor. "I wanted to keep it, but Mum said I was too young to cope, and Dad said we couldn't afford it."

"Too damn right," he spat. "Everyone who found out about it either laughed at her or called her a slag."

Mandy winced, and in that moment Wednesday felt for the girl.

"Do you know if his wife knew?"

"She did; I told her to her face," replied Ron, crumpling the paper in his lap. "I found out where he lived, and told her all about him. Poor cow was choked."

Mandy dropped into an empty chair, burying her face in her hands as she allowed simpering sounds to filter through her fingers.

"Did you see him after your meeting with his wife?" Wednesday asked.

"He's a coward. He didn't 'ave the nerve to confront me. He was in the wrong and he knew it. I bet he only pretended he believed she was older."

"Did he force you to have sex with him?" asked Wednesday.

The girl shook her head. "I loved him, and I thought he loved me. I wanted to keep his baby," she sobbed.

"What does a sixteen-year-old know about life? It's still playtime to them, but we adults know the meaning of hardship and graft. It's all pretend at that age. I'd 'ave been forking out for the kid left, right, and centre."

The sound of the front door opening and closing in quick succession alerted them all to a new arrival.

"Just in time, Tracy, it's the police about *that* bloke's death," said Ron.

Tracy took her coat off, revealing her Greg's uniform underneath. "I see you've managed to upset Mandy," she said finally. "What's his death got to do with us?"

"We're exploring every avenue. We've only just discovered Mandy's relationship with him."

"And you're assuming one of us killed him?"

"People have killed for less."

"Where were you on the night of his death?"

Tracy looked at the calendar on the wall. "Ron and I were at the social club, and you were out with your mates," she said to Mandy, who had finally stopped crying.

"Where did you go exactly," Wednesday asked the girl.

"We went clubbing to Tower's; I was hoping to see him, but instead he was getting killed." She burst into tears again as she ran from the room, with Tracy scuttling after her.

"See what he's done to her? She's no longer the bubbly girl she once was. If he wasn't already dead, I'd bloody kill him myself." He looked at them and shrugged.

Lennox took down the details of the social club before they retreated quickly to the car.

"Richie had a negative impact on many people's lives," Wednesday commented.

"Didn't deserve to die and have his tackle removed, though."

"Agreed, but I'm not sure what he achieved in life."

"Apart from making lots of women happy."

"Trust you to say that. Is that how you see yourself?"

"Thus far, I'd say I've made a lot of women unhappy."

"Maybe that's because you're unhappy, and until you change how you feel about yourself, you risk continuing the cycle."

"I'm tainted by the stupid mistakes I made in the past, and I wonder if I'll ever find a woman who'll ignore the stains."

"Maybe you need to travel further afield."

"Mores the pity," he said quietly.

Chapter 24

Scarlett was sitting in the dark at the kitchen table when Wednesday arrived home. She knew it was a bad sign. Instead of switching the light on, she lit the candles in the centre of the table.

"Fancy an Earl Grey?" she asked lightly as she filled up the kettle.

When her question was met with silence, she slid the kettle onto the Aga before sitting down.

"How's your day been?"

"Slow and painful."

"In what way?"

"The hours drag as though time itself is swamped by the thickest mud, dripping in slow motion from every second."

"And the pain?"

"Having the insight and realisation that our mother's madness lies within me. All these years you've worried about yourself, not seeing that it's actually me who's sliced through by the malady."

Wednesday stood up and made a pot of tea then brought it to the table. She placed a cup and saucer before them both, then sat down.

"I worry about us both," she sighed.

"I bet you've escaped it."

"We don't know that to be true."

"The chances of us both being mad must be slim."

"I was once on a case where the two eldest children had schizophrenia, and the third child had a personality disorder. The mother had tried to set fire to the home after discovering the daughter was pregnant. Shit happens."

"Poor Dad; he must have behaved badly in a past life."

"You don't believe that. He loves us all, no matter what happens."

"Mum's lucky, I'll never find a man like him."

"Someone somewhere will love you for you, regardless of what baggage you may have. You need to have faith."

"Easy for you to say."

"Why? I don't have anyone special."

"You've got Lennox by your side most days."

"Because he's my sergeant, not because he chooses to be."

"I bet he's glad we're not together anymore. I get the feeling he wouldn't tolerate travelling the skidding road to crazy town."

Wednesday laughed. "You never fail to amuse me, and that'll get you a long way, you'll see."

Scarlett buried her face in the shadows. "I hope to keep riding the highs, as the lows are so hard to bear. It's like standing on a precipice all the time, knowing that any tiny knock could send me plummeting into the darkness. I live in a dream world that could turn into a nightmare at any given moment."

Wednesday reached out, putting her hand on Scarlett's, but saying nothing. After a few minutes, she poured the tea, thinking how very British her action was.

"We'll get through this," she said, finally.

Scarlett's nod was almost imperceptible in the dark, but Wednesday sensed it all the same.

They remained in the flickering light, quietly sipping tea, letting thoughts, whether good or bad, drift back and forth across their minds, but never into their mouths.

Isobel Dover smelt the aroma rise from the cup of freshly brewed coffee before taking a sip. She closed her eyes and let a gentle smile lift the corners of her mouth.

The newspaper landed on her doormat with a thud. Getting up, she sauntered to the front door to see the outline of a figure through the stained-glass panel. Stopping in her tracks, she measured her breathing before walking up to the door and putting on the security chain.

"Who is it?" she called out.

"It's me, Jack, Jack Turner."

"What do you want?"

"I need to speak with you."

She picked up the paper before unlocking the door. Holding the paper in front of her like a shield, she smiled up at him. He stepped forward, entering the house with a sense of urgency.

"Have you seen the police recently?" he asked, brushing his hand over the top of his head.

"Yes, why?"

"Well I don't know what you've said to them, but they seem to think I murdered Richie to be with you. You know I'd do anything for you."

"And did you?"

"I didn't bloody kill him, if that's what you mean. I was happy to wait for the divorce to be finalised before . . . before making my move. But someone's gone and spoilt it."

"You put yourself in the guilty seat by being so obvious about your emotions."

"That's just what the police said. You're being a bit harsh, have I upset you?" He reached out to touch her shoulder, but she flinched away. "Are you frightened of me?"

"I don't know who to believe anymore. The police have intimated someone in the group is the perpetrator. How do I know you haven't come here to murder me?"

"Because I love you."

Shuffling back, she found herself pressed up against the wall. He gave a lopsided smile before bending down and putting his mouth to her ear, so she felt his warm breath on every curve.

"I can wait. You'll be mine one day; I'll make sure of that." He kissed her forehead before leaving her pinned against the wall in terror.

Wednesday sat next to Scarlett in the psychiatrist's stuffy waiting room. She was aware of the other people sitting around them, hoping they did not think she too was a patient. The thought hung heavily on her shoulders, and only lifted slightly when Scarlett was called in to see the psychiatrist.

Doctor Green's ginormous body hung over the sides of his chair, his belly bulging over his belt. Webs of broken capillaries lay across his bulbous nose and cheeks, and his beard had the remnants of a croissant sprinkled in it. Round spectacles framed his piggy eyes.

"This is Doctor Warren; he's a junior doctor on placement with me. Is it all right if he sits in on this appointment?" he asked, pointing to a young man in the corner.

Scarlett nodded, letting her eyes linger on him a tad too long.

"How have things been for you since starting the medication?"

Scarlett looked around the room. "I'm perfectly well at the moment, thank you," she said, smiling at the junior doctor by just slightly parting her highly-glossed lips. "Don't I look well?"

"Actually, you're wearing a lot of make-up for the time of day, and your clothes are quite revealing." He peered over his glasses as though speaking to a child about what she wanted for Christmas.

Scarlett turned to Wednesday, raising her eyebrows.

"I did try telling you this earlier, but you wouldn't listen," Wednesday said quietly.

"Nonsense," Scarlett said, her voice pitching higher at the end of the word. "You've always been jealous of my ability to get any man I want—or you want, come to that. It must still stick in your throat that I bedded Jacob, and you haven't."

Wednesday pulled her arms tighter around her stomach, smiling meekly at the psychiatrist. He shook his head imperceptibly, urging her not to react.

"I would like Doctor Warren to finish the assessment in the next room, whilst I have a chat with your sister."

Scarlett stood up quickly, smiling at the young doctor, who rose cautiously, leading the way through the adjoining door.

"We've met before," Doctor Green smiled, "when I was treating your mother a while back."

"I've been dreading something like this happening; do you think she'll be like Mum?"

"No two people with even a similar diagnosis will follow the same pattern, or suffer in the same way. They each have a different diagnosis so Scarlett will fluctuate more between mania and lows, whereas your mother hovers around depression more often than not."

"I suppose that offers hope."

"Her GP mentions she's moved back in with you as she wasn't coping alone, and he fears she's no insight into her behaviour or how she's feeling, making her a danger at times."

"She's coping currently."

"And what about at work?"

Wednesday dipped her head. "She hasn't been going, but hasn't told me that. She's pretending she's still going. I haven't told her I've found out."

"Perhaps you should tell her when the moment's right. She needs to address what's going on in her life if she's to recover."

"Is this because Mum's ill?"

"Genetic influences play a part; symptoms do tend to run in families. A person is more likely to develop symptoms if a close relative has a diagnosis of schizophrenia or bipolar, for example."

"Then I'm stuffed too."

"Not necessarily. You've not shown any symptoms up until now."

"Not that I'm aware of. But I could be like Scarlett and not have noticed."

"I'm sure you know someone who'd be quick to point out any idiosyncrasies."

Wednesday thought of Lennox and nodded.

"Scarlett will have insight at times, as will your mother. It can't be nice knowing that a crushing low will hit you sometime soon."

"She said as much the other day. What do I need to look out for with Scarlett?"

"Watch out for her struggling to look after herself, or holding strongly held beliefs others don't share, like being watched or having her thoughts read. The cycles of mania and depression can occur at fairly regular intervals, but it does vary with each individual."

He then asked her to wait outside until he had finished seeing Scarlett.

Half an hour later, Scarlett appeared in the doorway, complaining loudly about dying to get her fix of coffee and slice of cake. On another day her theatrics would have made Wednesday smile, but not that day.

Once home, Wednesday set about making a pot of coffee whilst Scarlett studied the leaflet on side effects in the box of new antipsychotic medication.

"And so it goes on," Wednesday whispered to herself.

Chapter 25

Wednesday put the phone down as Lennox entered her office.

"That was Orla Dwight, the scientist. She's done some further research, and narrowed down the belladonna to some possible sites which she checked out. She found a small patch of belladonna growing around the remains of an old folly, in the grounds of an estate. The new lord and lady were very accommodating, apparently."

"That whittles down the group," Lennox replied, watching her break a square of chocolate from a bar.

"Something on your mind?" she asked.

"No."

"Right, let's visit Carl Trott and Jack Turner; see how they respond to our newfound knowledge. I'll drive."

Winding a strand of her hair around her finger, Tamara waited for Carl's response.

"You want us to get married otherwise you'll go to the papers about my indiscretions with young girls, rent boys, and male threesomes. Why would you want to marry me with such a scabby record?"

"Because I love you, and I know that I can lead you away from all that."

"You like a challenge then."

"All women do," she smiled.

Carl climbed out of bed, pulling a dressing gown around him, and wandered over to the window.

"In the current climate of celebrities and sex scandals, this would crucify me. Why would you do this to me, if you proclaim to love me?"

"Because you're a hard man to pin down. I want you to wear the biggest wedding ring possible, so all your female clients can see you're taken."

"That won't stop them."

"But me sitting in reception here, when you open privately, will."

Turning around, Carl fixed her with a stare before speaking. "We should go and find an engagement ring, then."

Tamara squealed, rushing over to him and throwing her arms around his neck. "I knew you'd ask me one day; I just knew it."

Carl hugged her, his eyes wide open, scanning the ceiling.

When the doorbell rang, he untangled himself and rushed downstairs.

"Hope we're not interrupting," Wednesday said, gazing at his robe.

"What can I do for you now?" he grimaced, hearing footsteps skipping down the stairs behind him.

"Detectives, we've got news to tell you; we've just got engaged," Tamara said excitedly.

"Congratulations, I'm sure you'll both be very happy," smiled Wednesday, glancing at Carl, whose lips barely curled at the corners.

"We'd like to speak with you about a few things."

He let them in, requesting he and Tamara dress before sitting with them.

The detectives heard murmurings coming from upstairs; a frantic, heated exchange, turning into silence as the pair returned.

Carl's clothes were crumpled as though just picked up off the floor and thrown on, whereas Tamara looked composed and serene, as though all were there to hold court with her.

"Looking at our past interviews with you both about your leisure time, you both mentioned your favourite walk was along the river Ivel, culminating with lunch in the famous Nag's Head pub in Baldock. Correct?" Wednesday said, letting her eyes rest coolly on Carl's face.

"So?" he replied, matching her gaze for a few seconds.

"This would take you through part of the Newberry Estate, would it not?"

"As much as this is intriguing, I must ask you to press on; we have a ring to buy," Tamara chipped in.

"Could you tell us about your walk through the grounds? Where it leads you to?"

"Carl loved to imagine we owned the place," Tamara smiled. "We'd walk along the river towards to wooden jetty, before turning towards the house to visit the ruins of the folly. You can perch on a chipped stone bench and dream of days gone by."

"Did you take any souvenirs from the grounds?"

"What do you mean? Apart from broken pieces of stone, soil, and shrubs, there's nothing to take. We didn't go up to the house, if that's what you mean? Is that what you're implying?"

"We've a warrant to take your walking shoes to be tested."

"Take what you want, I just want to get going," Tamara urged as she got up to fetch the shoes.

She returned quickly and handed over the items.

"We can leave now. Enjoy ring shopping."

Carl grimaced, amusing Lennox as he thought back to his own bittersweet memory, shuddering.

Looking dapper in his pinstripe suit and maroon cravat, Jack Turner was clutching a large leather briefcase in one hand, and his mobile in the other, talking rapidly as he strode up to his front door. He was unaware of Wednesday and Lennox standing there.

He immediately stopped talking, shoving the mobile into his trouser pocket.

"Detectives, was I expecting you?"

"We'd like to discuss some information that's come our way," replied Wednesday.

Jack shrugged, turning the key in the lock and letting them in.

"We understand you recently sold Newberry Estate," Wednesday said, sitting down at the kitchen table.

"Yes, that was a little goldmine. Nice people who bought it. Why?"

"You're aware of the folly, right?"

"Sure, damn eyesore if you ask me. They'd do better getting shot of it and either build a new one, or return the site to garden."

"Your wife was poisoned with belladonna, and a small patch of it was discovered at the folly site."

It took a few seconds for the information to sink in.

"You can't possibly believe I poisoned her."

"For the house and dog; people have done worse for less."

"The public can walk through that section of the grounds, I wasn't privy to special access."

"You don't appear alarmed by this information."

"I don't even know what the plant looks like, and I wouldn't have wanted to get my nice suit dirty by crawling around in the soil to collect plants."

"We've a warrant to search your home for any evidence pertaining to this crime."

"Do your worst, Inspector, I've nothing to hide." He watched as they rifled through his wardrobe, checking his collection of shoes, and bagging those of interest.

Wednesday deliberately avoided eye contact with him as she checked under his bed, acutely aware that he was as in control of his emotions as the gel was in control of slicking back his hair.

An hour later, Wednesday felt they had all they were going to find of interest, and informed him that they were leaving.

"Hopefully this will be the last I see of you, until you come to inform me who actually did poison Michelle," Jack said before softly closing the front door behind them.

Chapter 26

After giving Alex the shoes for testing, Wednesday mounted the stairs to find the Incident Room buzzing until they saw her, when a laboured hush dampened the atmosphere. She looked around uneasily until her eyes rested on Hunter standing in the doorway of his office. He signalled to her to join him.

Hunter pursed his lips as she entered his office and closed the door, aware of the team staring in their direction.

"I'm guessing you haven't seen this," he said, throwing a newspaper on his desk.

Wednesday looked down to see an article on the murder in The Davenport Hotel, written by Scarlett Willow.

"She hasn't been at work for a while, I don't understand."

"Clearly journalists can work from home. What I'm angry about is the amount of details she's written down. This is an ongoing investigation, and the perpetrator has been given enough information to keep one step ahead of us."

"Is this your way of asking if I gave her some insider information, Guv? Because if you have to ask, we clearly haven't moved on much since I started working here."

"I've every right to continue supervising you; you do well to remember that."

"Hang on, is this about what happened, or didn't, between us?"

"Don't you dare suggest I'm transferring my personal feelings onto this. And for the record, I'd have expected more from you. I thought you of all people would have had more compassion."

Wednesday's shoulders sagged with remorse. She wanted to explain herself but he waved her out of the office with a sharp flick of his hand.

She returned to her office with burning cheeks and mounting irritation. Lennox was quick to follow her in, closing the door behind him.

"That looked intense. I presume it was Scarlett's article that sparked that."

"Have you read it?"

"It has her classic dark humour thrown in, but it's totally unflattering of us. Eileen Potter certainly got her message across in the interview."

"Give me a synopsis."

"She gives gruesome details of the victim's injuries and the poisoning. She calls us incompetent for not being able to find the killer in the small group of suspects. According to the hotel owner, we've hounded her and targeted the hotel vindictively. She equates us to a poor man's version of Agatha Christie."

Wednesday bit the inside of her cheek, hearing the words spoken by Scarlett in her mind; she always had a wicked sense of humour. Niall's would have liked the grisly details as they were likely to sell more copies of the paper.

"Well, let's put this to one side and focus on the case," she concluded, pulling a chocolate bar from her drawer, then throwing it back in unopened.

Maria Jones knocked on the door before entering with the post. The handwritten envelope on top of the pile caught Wednesday's eye, so she opened it first.

"Well, this is a turn-up, we've been invited to Carl and Tamara's wedding reception. Makes a change from a funeral."

"I'm your plus-one?"

"No, your name's on here."

"But I'd be your choice of plus-one, wouldn't I?"

She rolled her eyes before adding the date to her diary, and wondering what she was going to wear.

Opening her front door, Wednesday was greeted by the smell of burnt cake, making her heart plummet. She remained resolved to challenge Scarlett's work ethic at some point in the evening.

The kitchen was dusted with a fine layer of flour and blackened scrapings from the bottom of cupcakes. Scarlett was sitting at the table, equally as messy as the kitchen.

"Tea?" Wednesday asked, moving to the kettle without waiting for a response.

"I wanted to make you your favourite salted caramel cupcakes, but I forgot about them. It's these damn meds, I keep nodding off."

"The side effects of your new ones will dissipate as time moves on." She poured boiling water into the teapot. "I need to talk to you about your interview with Eileen Potter."

"Niall loved it, but I guess you don't feel the same."

"You're damn right. Hunter was apoplectic."

"Nothing new there. I'm only doing my job, which currently is more successful than yours, it would seem."

"I thought you hadn't been going into work."

"Niall agreed for me to work from home for a while, and I already had the notes of Eileen Potter's interview, so it was easy."

"Easy to slate the work I'm doing."

"Come on, sis, don't take it personally. Eileen was truly pissed off with the whole business, and let's face it, it's one of them, anyone can see that."

"If it's that easy, then save me some time and tell me who it is."

"I don't know all the players; you have the upper hand. Anyway, aren't you supposed to be looking after me, not upsetting me?"

"Your diagnosis is not a carte blanche to behave in any way you see fit. You still have to work within the parameters of what's socially acceptable."

"Well I can't always see the boundaries, that's what mental illness can do to one's mind. I'd have thought you'd know that."

Wednesday took a sip of tea, gazing at her ethereal half-sister over the rim of the cup. For years she had a thread of jealousy running through her mind, comparing herself unfavourably to such a beauty, but now that seemed like a wasted emotion.

"You're right, I'm sorry." She reached across and touched her hand. "I'll endeavour to be more understanding, but please could you see your way to being less damning of my work in the paper, I don't need Hunter on my back."

Scarlett giggled.

"Oh grow up." Wednesday blushed before allowing a smile to traverse her lips.

All eyes turned to Wednesday as she scurried through the Incident Room heading for her office. Closing the door, she sat behind her desk and took off her left shoe, rubbing her toes and already regretting her choice of footwear.

Lennox knocked at the door before entering.

"May I say purple suits you," he said.

"Court shoes don't suit my feet, sadly, so you can drive." She looked up at him. "Nice suit, but not sure about the lavender cravat; it looks like we've coordinated our outfits."

"Better than clashing," he grinned.

The small wedding party had already arrived from the registry office, and the happy couple were having photographs taken next to a gigantic flower arrangement in a bay window of the exclusive boutique hotel.

Wednesday's eyes were drawn to Jack Turner, standing in a corner watching Isobel Dover as she fussed with Holly's hair. Stella stood by their side, drinking champagne out of a crystal flute. When she caught Wednesday's eye, she beckoned them over.

"Are you allowed to drink?" she asked.

"I'd prefer not to."

"So you're here on duty, not as guests?"

"Guests, but during work hours. How did the service go?" Wednesday asked, standing a little taller.

"As good as they can be. The photographer from the local paper took far too many photos, though; he slowed things down."

Carl and Tamara finally moved to the large, round table, where they sat down. The silver cutlery glinted in the light thrown down by the chandeliers, as the strong sun streaming in through the windows hit the crystals. Carl quaffed a glass of champagne, putting the empty glass on the table, his eyes searching for more.

"I'm surprised to see you two," Megan said, taking the seat next to Wednesday.

"We were invited, it seemed rude not to accept. Besides, you're an intriguing group of people," Wednesday replied, covering the top of her glass when a waiter passed by with the wine.

"By that I'm assuming we intrigue you because of the crimes which you've still not solved?"

"We're close. How's life been for you?"

"We sold the house and split the money. I'm renting a flat not far from the clinic; not sure where Paul is now though."

"So the weekend with Carl and Stella worked."

"I guess so. Are you and he dating?" she asked, nodding in Lennox's direction.

"God, no."

"So he's single, great," she said, removing her thin cotton shrug, revealing her toned arms.

Wednesday smiled, turning her attention to Tamara who was soaking up the attention; she looked brighter than Carl, who was quaffing successive glasses of Champagne.

After the first course, Tamara got up and swished around the table, thanking each guest individually.

"I thought you two wouldn't accept, but I'm glad you did. I think you needed to see everyone in a brighter light, not the gloomy version they presented at the hotel."

"By everyone, I'm assuming you mean Carl, as he's really your only interest."

"You got me," she laughed, "my husband *is* my only concern." She moved around, patting Holly on the head as her tinkling laugh reverberated around the room.

The air was sticky thanks to the sun streaming through the windows. Wednesday removed her cardigan, hooking it over the back of the chair, before picking up the glass of sparkling water. She was aware of Lennox engrossed in conversation with Stella, a fact which seemed to pique Megan.

"Why is he single?" she asked Wednesday behind a cupped hand.

"You'd have to ask him."

"I would if I could get a word in edgeways. Stella's got her claws into him, but I bet he wants someone younger."

Wednesday swirled the water in the glass, suddenly wishing she still smoked so she could pop into the garden. Scanning around, she noticed Jack's attention fixated on Isobel, his face glistening with a fine film of sweat. She was oblivious to the attention as she played with Holly, who was beginning to get bored with the whole affair. When the starter finally arrived, the need to be sociable evaporated.

"Still never see yourself marrying?" Lennox asked, leaning in to Wednesday.

"Correct. What about you, would you marry again?"

"Not likely, although I would like more of a long-term relationship."

"You have plenty of choice."

"Not the choices I want . . ."

He was interrupted by Megan standing up and loudly slurring her words as she tried to wish the bride and groom luck, whilst waving her wine glass in the air. Everyone laughed with some embarrassment, until she vomited over the table and on the floor.

Chapter 27

Holly shrieked as copious amounts of vomit splattered her new princess dress and sparkly shoes. Wednesday moved towards Megan and sat her back down, holding her long hair away from her face as she continued spewing onto the floor. A waiter rushed over with a bowl and a pristine white towel.

"She'll dehydrate at this rate," Wednesday said, screwing up her nose at the sickly-sweet smell.

Isobel scooped Holly into her arms, retreating towards the French window, hoping to distract her in the garden. Stella followed quickly behind, her hand covering her nose and mouth.

Tamara stomped around the room, gesticulating wildly, and screeching at the top of her voice how her special day was ruined. Carl attempted to calm her, but she shrugged off his hand, blaming him for everything.

Wednesday noticed Megan's rapid heartbeat pulsating in her temple and requested a doctor, but the manager had beaten her to it. Within a short space of time, an ambulance crew entered the room and quickly began assessing the patient. Everyone watched, pale-faced as they took her away under a blue flashing light.

"Now what?" exclaimed Jack.

"We're going to go to the hospital now, but I want all of you to remain here until we ascertain what's going on," Wednesday announced.

"What do you mean by that?" said Carl. "Surely she's just drunk."

"I didn't notice her drinking excessively, did anyone else?"

People shook their heads and shrugged, avoiding eye contact with one another, and especially with Wednesday.

"We didn't pour it down her throat," snapped Tamara.

"I'm not accusing anyone of a crime, I'm just ascertaining what everyone saw," Wednesday replied calmly. "We'll leave now and get back to you as soon as possible."

"Ethylene glycol?" repeated Wednesday, as the hospital smell irritated her, provoking unwanted sentiments and memories.

"It's found in antifreeze," clarified the doctor, standing in front of her with his stethoscope slung around his youthful neck. "I had the tests fast-tracked, as I knew you'd want to know ASAP, as did I."

"Will she be okay?"

"She's only ingested a small amount, enough to make her ill but not kill her, luckily. We've stabilised her and are replacing fluids through an IV drip."

"So this is a deliberate act of poisoning which made her seem drunk."

"The symptoms can make someone appear inebriated; slurred speech and swaying, for example. Fortunately, the violent emesis and swift medical attention helped her survive."

"Can we see her now?"

"She's fragile and tired, so don't spend too long with her."

Megan's skin looked like paper, and deep blue crescent moons were lodged under her eyes.

"I've just been told," she said in a gravelly whisper. "Someone tried to poison me, and I know who. I need protection . . ."

Speaking seemed to drain her of energy, so they moved in closer.

"I've been blackmailing Carl, and this is his revenge, or hers," she wheezed.

"Who's her?" asked Wednesday.

"Tamara. She found out, and was originally on my side, but something happened, and they got married, and now I'm in here." Her head rolled to one side, revealing strands of hair plastered to her cheek with sickly-smelling sweat.

"What were you blackmailing him about?"

"His sexual preferences; he likes sex and group sex with young men as well as women. I found out about it in the clinic; he's had various STIs," she coughed. "He said it would ruin his career if all his diverse sexuality and infidelity came out." She pointed to a plastic beaker of dusty water with a straw in it. Wednesday held it in front of her, enabling her to take bird sips to moisten her arid mouth before turning her head the other way.

"They'll try again, mark my words. I said I'd leave the country when I had enough . . . money." She began sobbing. Salty tears trickled down the side of her nose, pooling in the corner of her mouth.

"It's a serious allegation you make against them, but so is blackmail," warned Wednesday. "We'll go and see Carl and Tamara now, but once you've recovered you'll face charges of your own."

As they walked out they heard Megan sobbing quietly.

As Wednesday and Lennox entered the lobby, the acrid stench of vomit still clung to the air. A woman in a white shirt and knee-length black skirt was liberally spraying the aroma of rose around the room.

As requested, all the guests had remained at the hotel. Wednesday dispatched officers to take their statements whilst they interviewed Carl and Tamara, who had booked the honeymoon suite, before driving to Cornwall the following day.

They waited in the garden room for the newlyweds to arrive, and Carl was the first to enter the room with an apologetic look on his face.

"Tamara's redoing her makeup. Perhaps you can start with me?" he said, crumpling into a chair.

"Has she calmed down?" Wednesday asked.

"As calm as she'll ever be. If I were a man who believed in omens, then I'd be in fear of today."

"You haven't asked how Megan is."

"Sobered up?"

Wednesday held on to her answer as Tamara entered, allowing her firstly to settle in the seat next to Carl.

"The hospital informed us that Megan was in fact poisoned with antifreeze. Fortunately, it was only a small dose, or we could have been looking at murder."

"Poisoned? Here at our reception?" Carl leant forward, cupping his head in his hands.

"Now who's the drama queen?" Tamara laughed. "But seriously, bad luck seems to follow us ever since you began working with this group. I blame you."

"Seems to be my new role in life."

"We have a warrant to search your room," Wednesday said, holding the piece of paper an officer had passed her in front of Tamara, who immediately ceased grinning.

"What are you looking for?"

"Megan informed us of her blackmailing scheme against you, Carl, and thought Tamara was on her side until the wedding. For that reason, we must undertake a search to find any trace of the poison. You can come up if you want, but only to observe, don't touch anything."

Carl groaned and Tamara blanched, watching for shifts in his facial expression.

The four of them mounted the sweeping staircase and headed for the bridal suite.

"Impressive," said Lennox, eyeing the four-poster bed.

Wednesday moved towards the dressing table, laden with expensive products and perfumes, which she opened and sniffed before carefully opening the drawers and searching through delicate underwear, whilst Lennox opened the wardrobe.

"If you tell us what you seek, we'll tell you where it is," Carl said, despairingly.

"They don't know what they're looking for," chided Tamara. "I've a good mind to sue you lot for depriving us of our wedding day."

Wednesday reached for Tamara's white satin clutch bag on the bedside table. Opening it, she found a blue garter, a packet of tissues, some breath mints, and a perfume bottle. Unscrewing the top rather than spraying it, she found it had a distinctive sweet smell.

"Smell this," she said, holding it out to Lennox.

"Reminds me of being in the garage with my father."

"I'd hazard a guess and say it was antifreeze."

Carl turned to Tamara, who was now standing by the window fiddling with the pearl necklace around her neck.

"Tell me this is some kind of mistake, that you're covering for someone else," he said finally.

"They know she was blackmailing us; why pretend anymore?" She moved to the edge of the bed, and perched on the end. "I wasn't trying to kill her, I just wanted her to know our threats weren't empty. I wanted her to leave us alone."

"You could have come to us," replied Wednesday.

"Then his secrets would have been made public—"

"What's going to happen to her now?" interrupted Carl.

"We'll bag this evidence and arrest her. She'll be taken to the station for further questioning. You can come too."

Wednesday took her by the arm and escorted her out as Carl watched on with lines zigzagging across his forehead.

Isobel pulled the nursery door to, so only a chink of light from the landing entered the room as Holly liked. Tiptoeing downstairs, she went to the fridge and retrieved a bottle of white wine.

"Would you like me to open it?" asked Stella.

"It's only a screw cap."

She proceeded to fill the two crystal glasses before handing one to Stella.

"Shall we move to the lounge to be more comfortable?" Stella asked.

"This has always been my favourite room. When Richie was alive, he'd have the lounge and I'd stay in here."

"Then it's time you reclaim the house back. He's gone, and all this is yours now. Come." Stella stood up with her glass in one hand, reaching out to Isobel with the other.

Sighing, Isobel took her hand and allowed herself to be led into the lounge. They sat in the tub chairs facing one another next to the fireplace, sipping wine.

"How am I supposed to tell Holly about what happened to her daddy?"

Stella took a sip of wine. "It won't be easy, but she'll need to hear it from you, not in the school playground. They'll all know her father was murdered; it's more than your average school-gate gossip."

"The thing is I didn't love him when he died, and I fear my lack of compassion will be misinterpreted by her."

"I could help you when the time comes, if you want."

"I think I'd like that, thanks."

They emptied their glasses, so Isobel trotted to the kitchen to fetch the bottle. On returning, Stella had gone. Thinking she was in the bathroom, Isobel poured the wine before curling up in the chair, cradling the glass between her hands.

Muffled stirrings whispered through the baby monitor. As they grew stronger, Isobel heard Holly say a few incoherent words, like those of a drunken person trying to order a kebab.

Curious, Isobel unfurled and crept upstairs. The nursery door was ajar just enough for a shaft of light to fall upon Stella sitting in the antique nursing chair, cradling Holly in her arms.

"Everything okay?" she asked, pushing the door open.

"I think it was just a bad dream, she's settled now."

Isobel took her child and tried placing her back in her cot, but having woken, Holly objected to the potential separation with all the power from her lungs.

Isobel rolled her eyes. "We'll take her down with us, she'll soon drop off again."

Holly curled up in the corner of the sofa, clinging to her patchwork rabbit, and wrapped in a cotton blanket. Her plump cheeks shuddering as she sucked hard on her thumb.

"This is all I ever wanted," Stella said quietly, raising the glass to her lips, with her eyes fixated on Holly.

"You never had children?"

"I was pregnant once, but my then-husband kicked it out of me. I was left with internal scarring, preventing any further pregnancies."

"Oh God, I'm so sorry." She hid her red face behind her wine glass.

"But it's not just Holly. It's you; it's everything. I've always wanted a family and a proper home . . ."

They jumped at the sound of the doorbell which was followed by rapid knocking on the door. Only Holly remained unaware of the intrusion.

"I don't expect anyone to call 'round uninvited after nine," Isobel sniped. "I'll send them away."

She walked to the door, aware of the distorted shadow she saw through the rippled glass panel.

"Yes?" she called out.

"Isobel, it's me, Jack. I need to speak with you."

"It's late. Can't you come back at a more sociable hour?"

"No, it has to be now, please."

Opening the door, the smell of alcohol hit her. He swayed slightly, clinging to the door frame with his left hand.

"I had to see you; I can't think of anything else . . ." he paused to concentrate on stepping inside.

"Did you drive here in this state?"

"Don't be cross with me. I can't function without alcohol, currently.

Talking with you will help."

He staggered behind her, blustering into the lounge to find Stella standing by the widow with Holly still sleeping over her shoulder.

"What's *she* doing here?" He pointed a fat finger in her direction.

"I've come to give Isobel emotional support. More to the point, what are *you* doing here?"

"None of your business."

"Take a seat. Stella will put Holly to bed, and I'll make us all a coffee," Isobel said, gesticulating wildly behind his back to Stella.

Jack crashed onto the sofa, whilst the two women scurried into the corridor.

"I think he may have come here to kill me because I rejected him," whispered Isobel. "I'm petrified, thank God you're here."

"He can't harm you, don't worry. I'll be back down in two seconds."

Isobel stood helplessly at the bottom of the stairs, watching Stella climb them two-by-two before disappearing into the nursery. She turned towards the kitchen to find Jack standing in her way. Her heart pounded so loudly in her ears she could not hear his words; she could only see him moving towards her.

"You need to be looked after; treated right," he slurred. "Richie was the biggest fool on earth to let you go." Reaching out, he stroked the side of her face, resting his hand on her neck. "I know you said you weren't interested in me, but I've done so much for you, and could do so much . . ." He stumbled forward onto her, before thudding to the floor.

Stella stood above him on the stairs, a heavy vase in her hand.

"My God, what have you done?" squealed Isobel.

"Shush, you'll wake Holly."

Bending down slowly, Isobel tentatively put her fingers on the side of Jack's neck. "I can't feel a pulse."

"You're probably doing it wrong. Anyway, what does it matter, he was a nuisance mooning around after you."

"We need to call an ambulance or the police or someone."

"There's no rush; it was self-defence."

"He was only stroking the side of my face."

"And you liked it?"

"Well, no, but—"

"No need to worry then. Come here," she said, moving down the stairs with her arms open.

Isobel stood rigidly, unable to mould herself into the embrace.

"What's wrong?" Stella asked, stiffly.

"I can't relax with a dead body in my hallway."

"Maybe we should drink some more wine. That's helped you before, remember?"

Sitting at her kitchen table, Wednesday stared at her mind-map sprawling over the surface. She sensed she was close to seeing who it was, but her mind fragmented the more she focused.

She stood up and wandered quietly into the lounge, where Scarlett was fast asleep on the sofa. She had become accustomed to sleeping there, even though she had a perfectly adequate bedroom upstairs.

Walking back out, she brushed against a repugnant vase of fake flowers Scarlett insisted on bringing with her. Rubbing the scratches on her arm, she walked back into the kitchen, returning to the carver chair.

Staring into the middle-distance, she reached across the table and pulled her phone from her bag.

"It's me, I'm coming to collect you in five. Be ready."

Chapter 28

Lennox only just managed to close the car door before Wednesday sped off.

"Call the station and tell them where we're going; we may need back-up," she ordered.

Lennox clung to the edge of his seat as he dialled one-handed.

Arriving in the street, Wednesday pulled up sharply. Jumping out, she marched to the door and rang the bell numerous times, looking up to see if she could detect movement.

"Okay, get back in the car," she snapped.

Reversing out of the space, she turned the car around and headed back into the city.

Finally parking up once more, she was relieved to see lights on in the house. This time, they moved more cautiously to the front door, listening intently in the peaceful neighbourhood.

Wednesday rang the doorbell and waited. She rang again, but still no movement from inside. She could see a light coming from the hallway, so bending down, she peered through the letterbox.

"I think we've got trouble; there's a body on the floor," she whispered.

Lennox took a look. "Looks like Jack Turner. What's he doing here?"

"The same as us, perhaps. Let's try around the back."

They pushed through dense overgrown shrubs, catching their clothes and hair on the prickly offshoots. The back was securely closed, offering them no opportunity for access.

"Let's get back to the front, and force our way in if necessary," she said, pushing her hands into his shoulder blades.

She rang the bell relentlessly before calling through the letterbox, saying they would ram the door open in two minutes if it wasn't opened. Lennox looked at her then his shoulder, shaking his head slowly.

"Maybe in my younger years," he whispered.

Distorted shadows moved behind the door before they heard Isobel's voice.

"It's very late. Please come back tomorrow."

"I don't think Jack Turner can wait that long," Wednesday replied.

"That was self-defence; and he's in no hurry, he's already gone."

"Let us in, unless you want the whole neighbourhood alerted to the situation; we still need to check on Jack."

A chain rattled before the latch clicked. Isobel peered through the tiny crack. "This isn't good timing."

"Is Stella in there with you?"

Silence answered her question.

"Let us in, we can help you."

Isobel giggled. "Help me? Why does everyone think I'm a helpless woman? Is it because I married a womanizer, and became a victimised stay-at-home mum?"

"No, it's because we think you're in danger."

Isobel unhooked the chain, and opened the door a little wider before letting them slip inside. They moved quietly and swiftly to Jack's body. Wednesday felt for a pulse, and located a faint one.

"Call an ambulance," she whispered to Lennox, putting Jack in the recovery position, and covering his body with a coat from the bannister. She glared at Isobel.

Standing up, she looked up to see Stella standing halfway down the stairs holding Holly in her arms, fast asleep. Isobel looked up at her.

"Why have you got Holly again, is she all right?"

"She's safe with me, you should know that. You're both safe with me.

Make these detectives go away, and we'll be the family we should always have been."

"We can't leave whilst Jack Turner's on the floor, and we need to speak with you both of the events that led to this," Wednesday said firmly, but cautiously, sensing tension in the atmosphere.

Stella hugged Holly tighter into her, disturbing the child who began to stir and whine.

"Give her to me," Isobel requested, moving to the bottom of the stairs and holding out her arms.

Stella took a step up, shaking her head. "She's precious to me, you know I won't harm her."

"She's precious to me too, and you're frightening me. Give her to me, now." Isobel's voice rose to a pitch of desperation.

Wednesday stepped forward, putting her hand on Isobel's shoulder. "Why don't you make some tea. Holly's okay, we're here."

Isobel moved away slowly, gazing at Holly until she could no longer see her.

"What are you expecting to happen now?" Wednesday asked Stella quietly.

"Isobel and I will raise Holly to be a fine young woman, possibly a counsellor like myself."

"Is Isobel aware of your plan?"

"Not in so many words, but she's not stupid. She's been bruised by her husband; she knows I'm the only viable and positive option for her and little Holly."

"Why don't you return Holly to her bed and then we can sort this out with Isobel over a cup of tea."

"Do you think I'm dense, Inspector? I sense you don't trust me and I'm not sure why."

"I was thinking back to the recent wedding; remembering how the room got hot after a while. We all removed our outer layers, but you kept your cardigan on with the sleeves pulled down."

Stella hugged Holly harder, who had woken fully and was protesting intensely at being disturbed. Isobel returned, looking wide-eyed between Holly and Wednesday. Wednesday lowered her eyelids slowly at Isobel before turning her attention to Stella once more.

"I was wondering if there was something wrong with the skin on your arms."

"No, why should there be?"

"In that case, could we take a look?"

Stella took a deep breath. "Don't you need a warrant?"

"Oh for goodness sake, show them your arms," Isobel said, moving to take Holly from her.

Stella moved up another step, with Holly now hollering in her arms. She struggled to maintain her grip, unused to holding a writhing child. Lennox moved swiftly, catching Holly as she tumbled from Stella's arms. Isobel darted towards him taking her from him before moving behind him by the front door.

"Show them your arms, and prove there's nothing wrong, *for me*," she urged Stella, who now had her arms wrapped tightly around her middle.

Pulling slowly at her sleeve, Stella revealed her right forearm, which was unblemished. She then paused before pulling on the left sleeve. Wincing, she dragged the fabric over her flesh, exposing clusters of blisters and burn-like marks.

"That looks sore," Wednesday said. "You should get some medical attention. How does your skin react to sunlight?"

"It hurts, why?"

"It's a nasty rash. The blisters will heal slowly, but you may have developed phytophotodermatitis, which is a rash that flares up in sunlight."

Stella gingerly pulled her sleeve down.

"What's this got to do with anything?" Isobel queried.

"We've identified the location where the belladonna came from, and giant hogweed also grows there. When skin comes into contact with it, it causes the rash."

"I'm always on country walks, I may well have come into contact with those plants anywhere; you can't prove anything from that."

"All the same, I'd like you to come to the station to let our forensic guy and doctor have a look at you."

Stella jutted her chin out, fleetingly catching Isobel's eye as she fidgeted on the stairs.

"Why the hell would I want to poison Michelle?"

Isobel took a sharp intake of breath then looked up at Stella. "Prove to them you're innocent. Go with them, if you've nothing to hide it'll be all right."

Stella frowned then gingerly took a few steps towards the group.

"Are you coming too?" she asked Isobel.

"I can't drag Holly to the police station at this hour. You'll be fine, don't worry."

They let the awaiting ambulance crew in to attend to Jack, then headed for the car. Stella slid into the back seat, staring straight ahead.

Edmond and Alex were waiting in the bowels of the building. As Wednesday passed the open door to the courtyard, the smell of cigarette wafted in the air. The smell was still nauseating, and she was glad she had remained smoke free.

"How are things progressing?" she asked, seeing the pair studying a photo closely.

"I believe we have the answers you're looking for," Edmond replied, peering over the top of his glasses. "The rash on Stella Hibit's arm is indeed phytophotodermatitis, caused by giant hogweed. I presume that's helpful."

"And the DNA sample is conclusive."

Wednesday smiled, thanking them before returning upstairs. Grabbing Lennox from his office, they headed to the interview room, where Stella was waiting for them.

"You don't have to hide your arm anymore; we know it's a reaction to giant hogweed, which grows around the belladonna you picked to poison Michelle Turner."

"I did nothing of the sort. Why would I?"

"The rash and opportunity say otherwise, but the *why* is thus far baffling," replied Wednesday.

"You have nothing on me."

"You ramble around the shires, taking photos of old churches and ancient buildings such as follies. Our detectives are currently retrieving the photos from your home to identify the locations. One location in particular."

Stella wriggled in the plastic chair. "I visit places anyone can visit."

"We've been delving into your past; I imagine you don't hold men in much esteem."

"And what of it?"

"I think men who are violent or unfaithful would be vermin to you. Some of the men in the group had done such deeds, did you find them hard to interact with?"

"I'm a qualified councillor; I'm trained to cope with being emotionally dumped upon, and to deal with people who challenge me personally."

"Most people in the group found Richie's behaviour distasteful. How about you?"

"The age difference between him and the girl made me cringe, I admit, but so what?"

"The post-mortem action was a very personal thing to do. Perhaps something only a woman would do."

"What of it?"

"We have evidence linking you to his murder."

Stella's cheeks flushed as she twisted her hands more frantically in her lap.

"The smell of coal tar often lingers around you. You suffer with psoriasis, don't you?"

Stella looked at her hands, the backs thin and puckered as screwed-up parchment. "A genetic hand-me-down from my grandmother."

"The shedding skin gets everywhere, doesn't it?" Wednesday tilted her head to get eye contact with Stella, who was still looking down.

"And fortunately for us, a tiny skin cell lodged itself between the base of the blade and the handle. Your skin cell, to be precise."

Stella's eyes glistened as she blinked rapidly. A salty droplet escaped, diving into her lap and soaking into her denim skirt.

"Did he remind you of someone from your past?"

"You wouldn't understand."

"Try me."

"Yes, Richie was no different from millions of cheating men, he was a serial offender which was allowed to manifest thanks to his so-called celebrity status." She sat back in the chair and raised her head.

"But you hardly knew the couple. Why the extreme reaction?"

"I met them prior to the weekend to assess their suitability for the Parting Ways sessions and I fell in love." She dropped her head once more.

"With whom?"

"With Isobel, of course."

Wednesday felt Lennox shift in his chair.

"You decided after one meeting you were going to kill the husband of the woman you loved. I find that hard to assimilate."

"Perhaps you've never been deeply in love. Perhaps such a profound emotion has eluded you, but it hasn't me. I feel my love for her to the very essence of my core. She opened up to me about the pain he'd caused her, both physically and emotionally, and I couldn't bear to see her like that."

"Is your love for her reciprocated?"

"It was on that Friday night in the hotel. After that, I knew what I had to do."

"Was Isobel aware of your plan?"

Stella paused, licking her parched lips.

"The question's simple, did Isobel know you were going to kill Richie over the weekend?"

"I told her not to worry, that I'd sort things out."

"What did she take that to mean?"

"The custody battle, the fabricated charges of her inability to parent adequately due to her drinking, and his violence towards her."

"How did she think you were going to do that?"

"She thought I was a brilliant counsellor, and that I'd be able to turn him around. I think she thought I could talk sense into Children's Social Services."

"She had faith in you, why do you think that is?"

"She said she fell in love with me at the same time I did with her. She said she felt safe and protected with me; that I offered her and Holly everything they needed."

"Did she elaborate on what she saw in the future with you?"

Stella chewed her lip. "She saw us as a family unit, growing old together."

"I think you're besotted with her. You'd do anything to make her happy and your dreams come true, blind to the consequences." Wednesday sat back, folding her arms.

Stella cast her eyes to the floor, refusing to enter into further dialogue. Wednesday was going to have to work harder. She leant in to Lennox before informing Stella they had to go. She stared back blankly.

Lennox closed the door behind them.

"Do you want me to drive?" he asked.

She nodded before dashing to fetch her bag. Out of the corner of her eye she spied Hunter watching her from his office. On another day, her red face would have embarrassed her, but today, there was no time to dwell on her reaction.

Holly was in the back of the car, whinging in the car seat. The boot was open, displaying a changing-bag and a rucksack full of toys. A vanity case perched on top of a bulging suitcase. Isobel was nowhere to be seen, but the front door was open.

They rounded the car and headed to the door. Wednesday called out to Isobel.

"Bloody hell, you frightened the crap out of me. What are you doing here?" snapped Isobel, appearing in the hallway.

"We thought you'd like to know, Stella Hibit has confessed to the murders," said Wednesday.

Isobel's eyes widened. "Stella, heavens, I didn't see that coming. Well done, you've solved the crimes. Maybe now I can get on with my life with Holly."

"When she gives us the absolute truth, maybe Holly will be the only one free."

"You intrigue me," she replied lightly.

"Stella's not a natural schemer or killer. She was blindsided into it on the false premise of procuring a loving family. An idea you put in her head."

Isobel straightened her back and smiled dryly.

"Without evidence, I don't see how I can be implicated. It's her word against mine." She stepped forward and sidled past Lennox on her way down.

"She won't like knowing you're free yet not visiting her. She'll feel betrayed sooner or later."

"If you say so. Now if you don't mind, I have to finish loading the car."

Watching her, Wednesday's shoulders felt crushed under the pressure of failure. Isobel was right, they had nothing.

Holly had fallen asleep by the time Isobel pulled up at the curb; she was glad of the peace.

When Carl opened the front door he stepped back into the shadows, forcing her to squint to see him.

"Are you alone?" she asked.

"Tamara's in the bath. What do you want?"

"You, of course; you must have been expecting me."

"Must I?"

"The time's right for us."

"I don't know what you're talking about, there is no *us*."

Her face reddened as her eyes widened. "What are you talking about? You've wanted me since the day we met at the initial interview. You were giving me come-to-bed eyes, and I knew you found me irresistible."

"You were imagining it. You were looking for affirmation from another man as your husband wasn't giving it to you."

"I've worked so hard to get to this point. If the idea of being a dad to Holly is off-putting, don't worry, you'll make a terrific dad."

Carl swallowed hard. "What do you mean by working hard for this?"

"I couldn't let Richie take Holly away from me, so he had to go, but I couldn't be the one to do it as I'd be an obvious suspect. When I saw Stella had feelings for me, I exploited that fact. I knew she'd give anything to have a ready-made family."

"You got her to murder Richie?"

She put her slender finger to her lips. "The less you know, the better. Now grab some things and come away with me; I've got plenty of money for all three of us."

Before he had time to answer, Wednesday appeared from the shadows from his therapy room doorway.

"What are you doing here?" Isobel asked breathlessly.

"You were clearly a woman with a plan, but a woman who relies on having a man at her side. A man with some form of celebrity or kudos to his name. Richie had the former and Carl had the latter. Lots of women have fallen for his charm and allure, why not you too? I thought when I saw you packing your bags that you may possibly call in on Carl to beg him to leave with you. You often mentioned your admiration of him."

Isobel's face blanched. "I don't know what you're talking about. This is all supposition."

"Apart from just hearing you admit to coercing Stella to do your bidding, we have a very upset and angry woman in custody. When we informed her you were packing up and moving away, and that you had no intention of being a family with her, she told us how you cajoled her into killing Richie for her, assuring her you'd be able to prove her innocence should the need arise." She took a step forward just as Isobel turned on her heels and ran straight into Lennox who appeared behind her.

"The stupid cow. Never trust a woman in love, she'll cut you dead if you dare to try and leave."

She jutted out her chin as Lennox led her to a waiting car and Wednesday removed Holly from the car seat.

"She was right about a spurned woman," Lennox said, clutching his bottle of beer. "They'll do anything to make you unhappy, and prevent you from moving on, even if they've found happiness with someone else."

"Are you talking about Lucy in particular?" Wednesday asked as she plated up three bowls of steaming spaghetti bolognaise, putting Scarlett's to one side for when she woke up.

"I suppose so. She's turned the boys away from me, and has made further involvement in their lives very difficult. I'm also wary of any future commitment with a woman that might come my way."

"But you've had plenty of women since her."

"You make me sound like a man-whore," he laughed. "All my encounters are transient sexual encounters with women I stand no chance of falling in love with as they're not really my type. I don't want to commit to a woman who gives herself away too readily."

"I thought that's how you liked it."

"I'm seeking a meaningful relationship with someone I can also share my day with, not just my bed. Much like we're doing now, I suppose."

"You'll find that special woman the day you stop looking for her. Stop pushing so hard, and just let things flow more freely. She'll come into your life when you least expect it."

Lennox took a large swig of beer. "I'm trying to be patient, but sometimes I'm desperate for things to move along faster."

"No woman is going to trust a serial dater; she'll need to know she's the special one. I did think you had that special connection with Scarlett at one point; I'm sure she did with you."

"Hell no, she was just fun for obvious reasons. No way could I see her being a permanent fixture in my life, or involved with my boys. I never actually loved her, it was just convenient lust."

In the shadows of the hallway, Scarlett stood like a statue, absorbing every word Lennox said; letting her damaged soul seep through her pores and melt onto the floor.

She slipped back upstairs and buried herself under her quilt, willing sleep to consume her and absorb the negative emotions ripping through her mind like a tornado.

Downstairs, Lennox watched Wednesday as she deftly wound strands of pasta around her fork, leaving flecks of sauce speckled around her mouth. He prodded his food before pushing the bowl to one side and taking another swig of beer, finally realising what a fool he had been. He contemplated the complexities of what happens after a man has loved unwisely, his toes curling in his shoes.

The case had also taught him a lot about the aftermath of divorce, and what happens when two people stop loving one another; or more precisely, what happens when one person stops loving the other.

Acknowledgments

Thank you, Peter, for trying hard not to interrupt me when I'm writing or editing. And thank you to Jessica "Goose" Kristie for her continued emotional support through author-angst moments, and James Koukis for all his editing prowess.

About the Author

Hemmie Martin spent most of her professional life as a Community Nurse for people with learning disabilities, a Family Planning Nurse, and a Forensic Nurse working with young offenders. She spent six years living in the south of France, and currently lives in Essex with her husband and a house rabbit. Her eldest daughter, Jessica, is studying veterinary medicine, and her younger daughter, Rosie, is pursuing a degree in computer science.

www.ingramcontent.com/pod-product-compliance
Lightning Source LLC
Chambersburg PA
CBHW020410210626
46816CB00006BB/2210